I0728444

BLACKWELDER 2164

Christopher D.J.

When it comes to hitting his target, Spencer Blackwelder can't miss. But when it comes to hitting the mark in other areas of his life, his aim is way off, which is definitely a problem when you're a military sharp shooter preparing for war with an alien species.

As penance for past mistakes in friendship and in love, Blackwelder makes the bold choice to relocate to Fort Felix, a military base on Neptune's moon, a decision that could end up costing him his life. Once there, he meets: Juan Miguel Arías, to whom he takes an immediate liking; Vernita Burton, a true friend; and the men and women of Brant Squad, a group of lovable losers that he eventually takes under his wing.

Blackwelder is surprised to discover he has something to live for again, but all of that is threatened when war finally arrives on Fort Felix's doorstep. Can Blackwelder find the hero within in time to save his squad, his planet, and the man he loves?

A NineStar Press Publication

Published by NineStar Press
P.O. Box 91792,
Albuquerque, New Mexico, 87199 USA.
www.ninestarpress.com

Blackwelder 2164

Copyright © 2018 by Christopher D.J.
Cover Art by Natasha Snow Copyright © 2018
Edited by: Jason Bradley

This is a work of fiction. Names, characters, places, and incidents are either the product of the author's imagination or are used fictitiously. Any resemblance to actual persons living or dead, business establishments, events, or locales is entirely coincidental.

All rights reserved. No part of this publication may be reproduced in any material form, whether by printing, photocopying, scanning or otherwise without the written permission of the publisher. To request permission and all other inquiries, contact NineStar Press at the physical or web addresses above or at Contact@ninestarpress.com.

ISBN: 978-1-947904-78-1

Printed in the USA
First Edition
January, 2018

Also available in eBook, ISBN: 978-1-947904-77-4

Warning: This book contains sexual content, which may only be suitable for mature readers.

Chapter One: Out of the Dark

"ALL RIGHT, JINX Squad, listen up," said First Lieutenant Robby Macke as he stood before Sergeant Spencer Blackwelder and the other crew members. "As you know, an abandoned Elumerian starship floated into the Barack's space sector forty-eight hours ago. It's been subjected to long-range and short-range drone scans, and we know that the propulsion and guidance systems are damaged beyond repair. There are several vacant exterior ports, suggesting the crew evacuated. Zero life signs on board. We are the lucky squad who get to be the first to dock with it. Our mission is to search the vessel, determine its threat level, collect any useful data, and return to the Barack. Any questions?"

"Just one, sir: with those giant sat dishes Miller uses for ears, there's no need for us to actually dock, is there? He can just conduct an audio scan from here," said Mudunuri. The other squad members laughed as Miller, the pilot, whipped his head around to shoot Mudunuri a scathing look.

"Is this the comedy hour? Or are we here to do a job?" Blackwelder asked. "Knock it off."

"Sorry, Sergeant Blackwelder."

Macke smirked. "Don't be absurd, Mudunuri; Miller couldn't possibly pull that scan off from here. He'd need to be, what, at least three clicks closer?"

Miller shook his head from the cockpit. The other soldiers sniggered.

"Lieutenant Abernathy, com check, if you please."

Abernathy adjusted her headset, then pressed and held a yellow button until it turned green. "This is Jinx Squad on Raider-1 to Barack actual. We're conducting a com check; do you read, Barack?"

"Raider-1 this is Barack actual, we read you. Coms are go, over," said a voice over the open channel.

Satisfied, Abernathy slid her hands along the console to a different cluster of brightly lit buttons. "Jinx Squad, internal com check, channel three. Confirm."

"Coms are go," they all said in unison. Over her shoulder, Blackwelder could see several lights flash green on Abernathy's console.

"Coms are go, Lieutenant," Abernathy said to Macke with a wink.

Raider-1 was a small ship with cramped quarters. There was a cargo hold beneath the floor of the ship, but its capacity was limited, not that they were expecting much of a physical salvage. Four soldiers shared the seating compartment with Blackwelder. Macke stood over the backs of the pilot and Abernathy, talking navigational tactics. They sat close together, their knees touching and occasionally banging into one another as the ship jostled. Several lit panels—some with loose-hanging cables—beeped above their heads. Expecting the atmosphere aboard the Elumerian ship to be completely inhospitable, the Allied Earth soldiers were wearing their space suits, sans helmets, and held their heavy-duty laser rifles at the ready.

The air was rife with tension; they had joked before, but Blackwelder knew it was a weak ploy to cover their mounting fear. None of them had ever stepped foot onto an alien, enemy vessel before. Blackwelder felt the concern himself, of course, but had to master it. Macke might have been the one giving the orders, but Blackwelder knew he'd be the one to keep them on point.

"Don't forget to breathe, Jinx," Blackwelder said to them all. "This is nothing more than a standard recon mission. You've trained for this." A couple of them nodded, but they seemed little put at ease by his words. He took a quick look at Macke, though the lieutenant didn't turn to meet his glance.

"And if any one of you shoots one of your own, I guarantee you you'll be eating nothing but veg-ox for a week."

A couple of them chuckled at the comment. "But what if you like veg-ox?" one of them said softly.

"Shut up, DeFrank," Mudunuri said.

"Target in range, LT. Better get strapped in," Miller said. On screen, Blackwelder could see a massive vessel that was rounded and bulbous on one end and through the middle, but that tapered off toward the tail. Cascading rows of spikes adorned the middle of the craft on both sides. The spikes, rounded at the edge and faintly glowing from their center, could almost be mistaken for fins. In fact, the whole ship had the look of a mutated whale, which reminded Blackwelder of the aquatic life they'd discovered years ago in some of Earth's more polluted oceans.

Macke nodded and turned to take his seat, the only available one being next to Blackwelder. Blackwelder looked up at Macke; he kept his expression blank, but inside he was laughing. He could see a moment of nervousness sweep over Macke's face, but he mastered it immediately and took his seat. Blackwelder couldn't help himself; he found Macke's discomfort utterly amusing. Raider-1 docked with the Elumerian ship shortly thereafter.

Macke stood up quickly from his seat and grabbed his helmet. "Miller, Abernathy, you stay with Raider-1 and monitor us. Mudunuri, you're with DeFrank. Pazmiño, you're with Sergeant. Blackwelder and Wine, you're with me. We'll split up, clear the ship section by section, and rendezvous on what we're eighty-seven percent sure is the bridge. Questions?"

Mudunuri opened and closed his mouth. Blackwelder could see the confusion mounting as he childishly raised his hand. "Uh, sir? Normally in the incursion scenarios, I partner with Pazmiño."

Jumping to his feet, Blackwelder cut across Macke before he could answer. "This isn't a scenario, dusties! In live missions, you take the orders given to you." He took a step closer to Macke and leaned in to whisper: "Though, sir, the familiarity of the old pairings may be an advantage for us in this situation. One less thing for them to think about. Unless there's a particular reason you want to readjust the teams?"

Macke glanced at Abernathy, who was close enough to overhear them. Her expression was quizzical, as she too seemed to be confused by the sudden change in the lineup.

"Besides," Blackwelder said, "it will be easier for me to keep you alive if I can watch your back."

"Yeah, okay," Macke said impatiently. "Old pairings: Mudunuri/Pazmiño, DeFrank/Wine, and Wellie, you're with me. Let's get in there and get this done, people."

BLACKWELDER AND MACKE approached a sealed doorway. They and the other members of Jinx Squad had been working for more than 90 minutes to clear the various areas of the starship, a task made more complicated by their inability to read the alien language that marked the corridors. Blackwelder brought up the rear as he continued to scan their periphery through the scope on his laser rifle. The helmet on his suit prevented him from bringing the scope as close to his face as he would have liked, but the screen had 3D technology that helped to compensate for the difference.

Macke reached for a panel near the door, one similarly placed to their own entry controls, but he hesitated. "Jinx Squad, check in."

"This is Wine, sir. DeFrank and I are just about to clear what appears to be a storage unit, and will continue moving starboard toward the bridge."

"This is Mudunuri. Pazmiño and I figured out their vertical transport system, so we've finished clearing the lower decks. We should be moving toward the bridge too."

Macke nodded in satisfaction. "Good work, everyone. The sergeant and I will rendezvous with you ASAP."

Blackwelder stared at the alien language printed above the control panel. "It's kind of freaky," he said, tilting his head to one side. The lettering was thin, slanted, and curved, but completely dissimilar to anything resembling Earth's linguistic characters.

"Yeah. We have no idea what's on the other side of this door."

"That's never stopped us before."

Blackwelder couldn't see Macke's face, but he could feel him rolling his eyes to dramatic effect.

Macke pressed a button on the panel, and as it had for several other rooms previously, the door slid open.

The room had a high ceiling with two large, dark pink circles in it. Blackwelder presumed from their experience thus far that they were the source of the light illuminating the room. The lighting had a different effect than Blackwelder had ever seen before; instead of streaming down from the source, and casting shadows in the process, the light seemed to brighten every item and person in the room individually. It was as if, instead of projecting light, they were absorbing darkness.

Along one wall were various computer stations. On the other, there were cubbyholes that contained small metal instruments. In the science fiction he'd seen growing up, humanoid aliens always seemed to travel in ships that were at least partly organic, with fleshy, slime-covered walls. But not the Elumerians. From what he'd seen, their designs were as clean and matter-of-fact as any Allied Earth ship. The overall shape of the room and corridors seemed to be more round and less angular than human ships, but that was the only real major difference Blackwelder could immediately detect.

Weapons at the ready, Blackwelder and Macke quickly moved across this new space, splitting to pass around two nine-foot tables planted in the center of the room. At the rear of the room, a pockmarked glass-like substance separated them from what appeared to be a collection of vialed liquids.

After poking their rifles in every conceivable corner, Macke finally said, "Clear."

"Clear," Blackwelder repeated, lowering his weapon just slightly. He made eye contact with Macke.

Macke held his glance for a moment before looking awkwardly away. "This appears to be their medical bay," he said stiffly.

"I'd agree with that. I'll check the computer, see if there's any data here we can salvage."

"Good call." Macke walked back toward the entrance of the room as if to keep watch.

Blackwelder pulled a data-sync disc from his pocket. It was thin, circular, and translucent black. He placed it against one of the monitors and it immediately adhered itself. Thin strokes of red outlined intricate circuitry detail that had previously been invisible, and then, like a spreading virus, the lines extended onto the screen. Fortunately, smarter people than him had designed the disc to worm its way into locked and encrypted systems and automatically retrieve data, so all he had to do was wait for it to finish its work.

He turned to Macke. "So, are we gonna talk about it? Or are you just gonna keep being weird?"

Macke whipped around, his expression deadly serious. He pointed toward his neck, where a green light shown on his suit. He tapped it twice, and it began to slowly blink. Blackwelder did the same.

"What do you think you're doing? We were on an open channel!" Macke said.

"I figured you'd switch us to internal coms. Just trying to get your attention."

"This is neither the time nor the place, Wellie," Macke said as he paced near the entryway.

"I would agree, *sir*. Except you're letting it affect you on-mission. So clearly we should discuss it."

"I don't know what you're talking about."

"Switching the lineups around last minute? Are you trying to get them killed? We practice them in pairs for a reason, to develop certain routines. Routines they fall back on when they get nervous or scared, not that I should have to explain this to you right now. Who knows what we're going to run into on this ship?"

"Well, I wouldn't be affected if you wouldn't keep flirting with me."

"I am not flirting with you! We're combing the halls of an *alien ship*, the first people on the Barack to do so, definitely, and probably some of the few humans to do it ever! This is terrifying and amazing, and despite the seriousness of the situation, I'm kind of having fun. And I'm here with one of my best friends!" He pointed at Macke. "So if you catch me with a smile on my face, or I'm *looking* at you, or whatever, it's not because I'm flirting with you. I'm just excited."

"Oh. Well, I guess that's fine. Yeah, I guess it is pretty exciting." Macke looked around. "Look, I just didn't want you to get the wrong idea, okay? It was just a one-time thing. An accident. We were drunk."

"The first time we hooked up was an accident, yes. But the *second* time was pretty intentional, on both our parts."

Macke narrowed his eyes, his body adopting a much more defensive posture.

"Calm down, Mack. It was a just a little fun between friends, all right? No big deal. It's not weird unless you make it weird."

The data-sync beeped, indicating that it had completed its task. The distraction was timely as it allowed a welcomed release from the tension. Blackwelder pocketed the data-sync and moved toward the door.

"I'm just saying, though—if you wanted it to happen again, you wouldn't necessarily need to get me drunk first. And just so you're clear, *that* was me flirting."

Macke moved his mouth as if he we about to speak, but before he could, Blackwelder slapped the blinking green light on his collar.

"Raider-one, Lieutenant Macke and I have cleared the med bay. We are heading to the bridge."

"Copy that, Sergeant Blackwelder," Abernathy said.

Blackwelder smirked at Macke as he exited. He brought up the rear once more as he and Macke entered the bridge. Mudunuri, Pazmiño, DeFrank, and Wine were already there. At the sight of their commanding officer, Mudunuri shot up out of the captain's chair, where he'd apparently been pretending to helm the ship.

The bridge was unlike anything Blackwelder had previously seen. The captain's chair, large enough to fit a being twice Mudunuri's size, was positioned at the far front of the bridge, nearest the view screen. Every other panel and console and workstation fanned out behind it like a two-dimensional pyramid laid flat. The alien command center was as spotless as the med bay had been, but the metal used in the command center was iridescent, the colors shifting between shades along the aquamarine scale. Aside from the captain's chair, there were no other seats; for a moment, Blackwelder felt a twinge of sympathy for an entire command crew being forced to stand throughout their shift.

DeFrank was busy at a console along the wall. She produced a data-sync similar to the one Blackwelder used in the infirmary and pressed it against the monitor.

"Data download commencing, sir," DeFrank said. "We should be all done here in about—" She was cut off by a sudden blaring. The thin lines extending from the disc that were once red now turned green, and the disc itself turned white. An alarm sounded, and as it echoed through the halls of the empty ship, the vibrations gained potency until they returned to Blackwelder with an intensity that curled his toes inside his boots.

Blackwelder pressed his free hand to his ear in a vain attempt to dampen the sound. "The command core data must be on a different security system. It's guarded against unidentified access."

In front of the captain's chair, the view screen came alive, flashing three-foot-tall letters in the alien language.

"Macke, I don't know what you all are doing in there, but we're getting some strange readings on Raider-1," said Abernathy.

"We've tripped an alarm," Macke said. "This place is going crazy, and we've got a pretty ominous-looking message on screen. What can you tell us?"

"According to the scanners, all of the starship's available power is being transferred to the engine core, and it's reaching critical mass. I don't speak Elumerian, but I'm pretty sure that writing you're seeing is a self-destruct countdown. Get your asses back here!"

"You heard her! Let's move, people!" Macke yelled.

Once they'd exited the bridge, Jinx Squad found themselves back in the main corridor, a large hallway with bright white track lighting running along the floors and around the windows that neatly framed the glittering expanse of space just outside the ship. On the wall across from the windows, circular light sources like the ones Blackwelder had seen in the medical bay were separated by what appeared to be the letter V molded into the wall. But as the blaring alarm grew louder, the white lighting slowly turned to a neon green color, which dimmed the corridor considerably. Little dots on the Vs began to flash green as well, in time to the breaks in the alarm.

As fast as they could, the team ran, skidding into walls and doors and stacks of containers that had long since lost their purpose, while the maleficent countdown glared ominously around every corner from screens Blackwelder had assumed to be inactive on their initial pass. The alarm morphed into a shrill whistling sound that reverberated through the halls at regular intervals; Blackwelder knew it signaled their doom if they didn't quickly reach the lower deck aft airlock, where Raider-1 was docked.

As they ran, one of the doors behind them slammed shut. Before they could register what had happened, another corridor sealed itself. Filling with dread, Blackwelder turned to his right, where the pathway would eventually lead past the medical bay that he'd explored earlier. As he looked on, two metal doors slid from their hiding places and slammed mercilessly in his face.

"The ship is sealing itself. They're trying to trap us inside." He had known that to be true from the moment the first door closed, but it wasn't until he said it aloud that he truly understood, and that understanding was followed immediately by a very real sense of fear.

"This way!" DeFrank yelled, shoving Pazmiño and Wine toward an open entryway on their left. With only a few sources of the sickly green light to show the way, they ran down yet another hallway, this one crowded by large metal cylinders. Blackwelder noticed there was some sort of liquid inside the containers, and that it sloshed about inside as the containers themselves hummed menacingly. The corridor came to an end at a sealed door.

"Dammit, DeFrank! You've led us to a dead end!" Mudunuri shouted.

"Wine and I passed by here on our initial sweep; the water reclamation systems are through this door. We can cut through the facility to get to Raider-1!"

Wine nodded aggressively in agreement. "It's wide open in there, so no random doors to get in the way."

"Well, let's get this door open," Macke said.

"Jinx Squad, switch laser rifles to full-power high-focus. Concentrate your fire on me," Blackwelder said. He raised his rifle, made the power adjustment, and squeezed the trigger. A dense red blast collided with the door, just inside the seam that sealed it to the wall. The metal sizzled and began to glow.

"Fire!" Macke ordered. The rest of the squad joined Blackwelder, concentrating their fire on the same spot. In seconds, the door began to melt away from the wall. As one, they slowly moved the beams up and down along the seam, until they'd broken through completely.

"Spacer!" Macke ordered. Pazmiño pulled a flat-bladed gadget from her pack and inserted it into the space between the door and the wall. The blades split into two and elongated rapidly, pushing the door open and clearing their way forward.

Once through, Blackwelder looked up; standing before him was a water tank stretching fifty feet into the air and wider around than his entire crew. And there were hundreds of them dotting the landscape of this area, the already dim green light made more eerie by the steam escaping from the vents placed all over the floor.

"The core's almost critical!" Abernathy yelled over the coms. "You've got minutes at most. Get here, now!"

And again, they ran. They blindly darted around tankards, following DeFrank and Wine. Blackwelder was bolstered by the confidence-increasing blip on his com that let him know they were approaching Raider-1. At last, they reached another door, and as promised, the view screen next to it indicated that they'd reached the airlock. Repeating their previous tactic, they melted the edge of the door and returned to the chamber where they'd first set foot on the Elumerian ship.

Macke grinned and gave DeFrank a pat on the back. "We made it. Open the airlock, Miller," Macke said. But when nothing happened, he looked concerned. "Miller? Get this thing open so we can go home."

"I can't! The remote access isn't responding. We're completely locked out."

"No, we're completely locked *in*. Get us out of here, Miller. Abernathy?" Macke said.

Abernathy shook her head. "It's no use, Mack. We can't get that door open from here."

Wine reached for his laser rifle. "Let's melt it!"

"It's an airlock, you idiot; it's far too thick for that," Mudunuri said.

Blackwelder quickly scanned the contents of his pack. "Likewise, I don't think we have enough personal ordnance to blast through it."

Macke hesitated, then nodded to himself a couple of times. "Then you'll have to blow it from the outside, Raider-1."

"Are you insane? Sir," DeFrank said, quickly correcting herself. "The explosive decompression could kill us all."

Macke looked around the room. "We'll be fine. Our suits will hold. We just need to strap ourselves down."

"But sir—" DeFrank began.

"We don't have time to argue this, Corporal! This ship's gonna blow in a matter of seconds. The only question is whether you still want to be in this room when it happens. Now strap yourselves down!"

Blackwelder pulled a towline from his suit's belt pack and wrapped it around his waist and arm before looping it several times around one of the chamber's support beams. The rest of the squad quickly followed suit, and once they were all secured, Blackwelder nodded to Macke.

"Miller, blow the airlock now!"

Miller decoupled Raider-1 from the alien ship and moved it a safe distance away. Then, he turned and lined Raider-1 up with the airlock.

"Raider-1, firing in three, two, one...."

A torpedo rocketed from the small craft toward the alien ship. Inside the airlock, the impact was marked by a deafening explosion. A monstrous, purplish-orange fireball reached out of the cosmos like the hand of God as the air inside the ship briefly ignited. Deadly projectiles rushed toward them, mirroring the torpedo's speed and intensity. Miraculously, none of them were harmed, but a sharp metal fragment embedded itself in the support beam where DeFrank and Wine had secured themselves, severing both of their lines. Helpless, the two soldiers were sucked toward the fire-tinged onslaught. Macke reached out and was just able to grab Wine's hand, but no one was able to reach DeFrank in time. The wave of light and heat from the explosion washed over them, and once it had subsided and the vacuum of space had reasserted its dominance, DeFrank was nowhere to be found.

"DeFrank!" Wine yelled, twisting in Macke's grasp.

"She's gone. And we've got to get to the ship," Macke said sternly, glancing over at Blackwelder.

Blackwelder released his rifle and, shooting quickly, cut each individual's mooring with a focused laser blast before severing his own. Jinx Squad began to float aimlessly in the normalized microgravity. Pazmiño flipped around end over end now that she was cut free.

Macke flipped a switch at his belt and his position was righted, as if he were standing on solid ground. "Rotational stabilizers on!". The others did the same. "Miller, open the lock."

"We're not going to make it..." Miller's voice was shaky. "There's no time."

"Miller! Open the damn lock!" Macke demanded. "The rest of you, activate your Man-U's. Full thrust. We're going to zip right into the cargo hold. Miller, the second we're in, you jump. You got it? Miller!"

"Yes, yes, got it."

"We can pressurize the hold, but everything down there now will get vented," Abernathy said.

"Better some random supplies than us. Blackwelder—" Macke began.

"I got the rear. Let's go!"

Macke clicked a control on the inside of his right forearm, and two small holes opened on his upper back. Nitrogen shot from the openings, propelling him forward toward Raider-1 with a jolt. As the other members of Jinx Squad activated their maneuvering systems, Raider-1 realigned and dropped its rear-landing platform. As it did, several crates flew out of the opening and then drifted listless into space.

Macke was zooming toward Raider-1. Mudunuri and Pazmiño were close behind, but Wine was flipping in a spherical pattern rather than being pushed forward. Blackwelder switched his Man-U to manual control. He was still sharpshooting, except he would make his body the bullet. After carefully timing his thrusts, he shot forward quickly, catching Wine in a perpendicular position and forcing him forward. He felt the nitrogen racing to escape from his back, a sensation that reminded him of being shoved repeatedly by a large schoolyard bully. Wine's arms were flailing, but Blackwelder could just make out Macke and the others narrowly making it into the cargo hold. Now it was his turn, and he knew this shot would take considerable skill.

He took a deep breath, calculated the distance still left between them and Raider-1, and deactivated his stabilizer. As he sensed his body becoming disconnected from the invisible restraints forcing him to stand upright, Blackwelder leaned forward and gripped Wine's shoulder, effectively pulling them both into a "flying Superman" position. With the combined effort of both their Man-U's, Blackwelder and Wine shot headfirst into the hold, where Macke was already waiting next to the auto-lock controls. Blackwelder crashed into Mudunuri with a painful thud, but he heard the hold slam shut behind him.

"Jump jump jump!" Macke yelled.

Raider-1 hummed loudly for a moment, and then there was a sound like bass dropping. Blackwelder was familiar with the tone, as it accompanied a ship jumping into hyperspace. He knew they'd vanished on the spot, leaving behind only debris to mark their former position. Still lying on the floor, Blackwelder finally relaxed and closed his eyes. They couldn't have been more than a second away from witnessing the Elumerian ship being destroyed in a violent explosion that would have sent pieces of the vessel soaring through the darkness in every direction. They'd narrowly escaped with their lives. Well, most of them had.

Chapter Two: Turn the Third Wheel

BLACKWELDER STOOD BEHIND the upper railing on the observation deck of the AES Barack as he admired the scene. At this distance, Saturn's girth took up about a third of the view. He'd been coming to the deck with a lot more regularity, determined to take full advantage of the respite in their raging war; the Elumerians had been relatively quiet since their flagship had been destroyed and they'd retreated just beyond the reaches of Neptune. Despite this, Blackwelder knew they would not be spared; losing DeFrank those months back had confirmed that for him. It was 1900 hours Standardized Earth Time, but Blackwelder's face was as fresh as if he'd just woken up, his dress browns as pressed as if they were newly dry-light cleaned. His reputation for being the best-dressed enlisted man in the Allied Earth Forces was well deserved. More so, given what he had to work with.

Below him, about a half story down, he noticed two enlisted soldiers, a male and female, sharing an intimate moment as they gazed at the vastness of space. They seemed so happy to be with one another. In public. In the relative privacy of the deck, which, granted, was walled in with floor-to-ceiling glass, but in view of other people nonetheless. Blackwelder sneered at them despite himself.

Macke walked up behind him. "Don't know why you keep coming here."

Blackwelder snapped to attention. His hand flew to his brow and froze there as if his whole body had been cast in iron.

"You've seen one of the Solara-Neuf, you've seen them all," Macke continued.

"Sir." Blackwelder's salute was picture-perfect.

"At ease, Sergeant." Macke sighed. "You're so formal these days."

Blackwelder considered Macke for a moment. He had the effortless charm of a six-year-old boy: every joke he told was the funniest, every adventure he had was the most exciting, every compliment he paid the most endearing. A wink and smile later, Blackwelder felt giddy, as if every happy memory from his childhood had flooded back to him en masse. Then he took a quick glance around, and the wellspring of joy he'd felt dried up immediately, leaving him cold. He had to remember that he was in public. He wasn't like the couple below him.

He turned away from Macke and faced Saturn. "I come here *because* it's still the same. Everything changed so fast after the first attack: the Global Peace Pact finally bringing us under one government...actual spaceships battling in the void? Like something right out of a movie. Even the sky is different. Home will never be the same after what they did to the moon." Blackwelder slumped down a bit on the railing. "Who knows what damage the next major incursion might cause? Gotta appreciate the beauty of the Solara-Neuf before they all get blown to hell. We are none of us safe, after all."

Macke rested one arm on the rail next to Blackwelder and slung the other arm over his shoulder. He leaned in close. "See, that's what I love about you. You're so sentimental." Macke's eyes glistened mischievously.

Blackwelder pushed Macke's arm off. "Don't do that."

He left Macke and walked toward the far end of the deck. Where the hull met the shatterproof expanse of glass, there was a somewhat narrow archway that led back to the 2030, the Barack's on-board bar and principal point of post-work shift convergence. The day was only just winding down, so the boozehounds hadn't made it out yet. Through the glass wall, Blackwelder noted that there were only two bartenders prepping glassware and one or two patrons who were clearly too absorbed in their own lives to notice him. Not that they could hear him at this distance anyway.

Macke caught up and grabbed Blackwelder by the elbow. "Hey, don't do what?"

"Don't put your arm around me and then look at me like that."

"Like what?" he said innocently.

"We're in public, remember?"

Blackwelder reached the very end of the deck. On the hull wall was the image of a giant globe with two Lego-like hands, one yellow, one brown, almost touching, the letters A and E displayed in the center in huge block font: the symbol of the newly Allied Earth. He leaned his back against the wall. Macke took up the space next to him.

"Being in public's not a big deal as long you don't make it a big deal," Macke said almost imperceptibly while scanning his periphery.

"Well, I'm sorry I can't be as subtle as you." Blackwelder was careful to keep his volume in check. "When you look at me like that, it makes me want to kiss you. And if I kiss you, here," Blackwelder indicated the wide-open space of the deck, "and word gets back to Hanson and the admiral, I'll be scrubbing toilets for the rest of my military career. Or until I get blown up by aliens. Whichever comes first."

"That's not true."

"Maybe not for you. I could take a picture of us having sex, blow it up, hese it to this globe, and almost everyone on this boat would still deny it. 'Not Macke. Can't be.' Hanson's a master at only seeing what he wants to, even if it's glued to a wall right in front of him."

"You're exaggerating. You're the best damn marksman in this command."

"That makes a difference to you and exactly one other person. Not to the people running this ship. And you know that."

"You're a well-respected NCO, Wellie."

"Only so far as I manage to keep you out of trouble."

"You know, you're being a real downer right now." Suddenly, Macke's forearm began to ring. He touched two fingers to his arm just below the crook of his elbow and slid them toward his wrist. A view screen appeared. "It's Lyta."

"Ah. Well? Are you going to answer it?"

Macke slid his fingers back toward his elbow, and the screen vanished. "I'm with you right now."

"You're with me." Blackwelder shook his head. "I wonder what your new fiancée would have to say if she knew you were 'with me.'"

Macke's eyes flashed dangerously. Blackwelder suspected, for a moment, that he might have to put his expert marksmanship to use, but then Macke's look dissolved into a playful smile.

"Let's grab a drink."

Blackwelder and Macke had downed several drinks by the time the bar began to fill up. Blackwelder looked up from his vodka tonic and saw a steady stream of soldiers, officers and enlisted alike, as well as the Barack's civilian crew, filing into the 2030 in earnest. Some had come from the mess hall, some were just finishing their shift, but they all looked like they were ready for a drink. One officer in particular waved to Blackwelder, and then made her way over.

Lyta Abernathy was a Disney princess: usually the cleverest person in the room, bold beyond her years, beautiful, and motherless. On their first night together in boot camp, she'd told Blackwelder how she joined the Force to escape an abusive home life back in the European Union. She'd said it with a muted smile, showing off a hard-fought self-confidence that made Blackwelder doubt that she had any regrets. He was impressed by the way she faced each challenge, somehow secure in the knowledge that everything would work out in the end.

"My two favorite boys. Should have known you'd be here, together. And you've started without me, I see." Abernathy nodded toward their nearly finished drinks, then gave Blackwelder a hug and a quick peck on the cheek.

"Sorry, babe," Macke said. "Wellie and I were just hanging out. You know, a little guy time."

"Right," Abernathy said. "More like 'guy on guy' time." She sauntered over to Macke and plopped down into his lap. The cheap chair gave a dangerous groan but held steady. "Hello, my love."

"Well, hello…" Macke and Abernathy's lips met, and it was like the entire bar dimmed in deference to them.

Blackwelder stared into his drink. He was afraid that he wouldn't be able to control his expression if he looked at them straight on, sitting there, being so open—like the couple from the lower deck. Blackwelder thought of Saturn's rings instead.

"So did you make captain today, my love?" Macke asked.

"No, not today. Though, grapevine has it Hanson and the admiral are still buzzing about that coded message I deciphered, about the Elumerians possibly preparing to regroup in Neptune space. Admiral Vaughn has convinced them to redouble our efforts on Triton."

"Triton," Macke blurted. "The moon colonies are the worst. Practically a death trap."

Abernathy nodded and then reached down for Macke's beer and finished it off in one quick swig. Blackwelder was still looking in every direction except at the couple, though as inconspicuously as possible.

"Well, you're awfully quiet over there," she said.

"Just got a lot on my mind."

"Hm. Like Trey Licata?"

"Lyta!" Blackwelder said, blushing but also smiling.

"Wait, Licata? The new mechanic? You two…"

"No!" He withered under Macke's gaze, feeling apologetic. Macke's eyes narrowed.

"But they could," Abernathy offered. "He's hot, Wellie!"

"But he's not gay," Macke said.

"As far as you know. You didn't believe me when I told you Wellie was gay either, remember?"

"Boy, were you right there." Macke seemed to remember himself the moment the words escaped his lips, but it was too late. Blackwelder shot him an icy glare that Macke reluctantly met. Abernathy, for her part, looked back and forth between the two, trying to interpret the unspoken as if it were just another alien code. She finally slipped from Macke's lap into the chair next to him.

"Anyway, let's talk about this engagement party," Abernathy said. "I'm so glad you're gonna help me with this thing."

Thankful for the break in tension, Blackwelder managed a small smile.

"Look, Lyta, just because Wellie's of the queer kind doesn't mean—"

"That's not why I asked him, Mack. It's because he's got the best taste of anyone in this fleet. If I asked you for help, I'd be stuck with Irish Car Bombs at the mess hall with cut-up old White Papers as streamers."

They all started laughing, a small, intimate laugh at first, that slowly grew into a roar. The three of them were laughing so hard their eyes watered, Macke suddenly in danger of falling out of his seat. Blackwelder wasn't sure where the sudden fit was coming from, but it felt great, and it was obvious they all needed a break in the tension. Blackwelder steadied himself, gazing at his two friends. He realized then that he would miss them both terribly.

Colonel Hanson, the second-in-command aboard the Barack, appeared suddenly behind them. He cut an intimidating figure, with his broad shoulders, thick neck, and heavy brow. "Well if it isn't the three musketeers! Macke, Wellie, and Abernathy. Together as always!"

"Sir!" the three of them yelled in unison, jumping to attention.

"At ease, all of you. I heard the news, Macke! Just wanted to come over and congratulate you two fine officers in person!"

Macke shook the colonel's hand vigorously. "Thank you, Colonel Hanson."

"And our prize code cracker! You're gonna make the prettiest bride this ship has ever seen." Colonel Hanson leaned in for a hug. Abernathy obliged, leaving the old man with a kiss on the cheek as well. "Set a date yet, young lady?"

"No, sir. I'm still trying to fumble my way through this engagement party I'm supposed to be having."

"Well, I don't wanna pressure you kids, but I would think sooner than later might be best. If your intel's correct, Lieutenant, and we have every reason to believe it is, the 'quiet' days might be long gone here real soon. I'd hate to see anything get in the way of your special day."

Macke grinned. "I have a deal with God, sir; we're covered until at least a week after the honeymoon."

"I bet you do, you slick bastard!" Hanson said, pounding Macke on the back.

Hanson turned to Blackwelder. He tried to look relaxed, although he was uncomfortable. "You ought to get yourself one of these fine young ladies too, son. Folks 'round here might start to get the wrong idea about you." Still smiling, Hanson playfully clapped Blackwelder on the back, who was trying very hard not to take the joke as the accusation he knew it was meant to be.

Macke glanced nervously between Blackwelder and the colonel. "Uh, buy you a drink, sir?"

"No, no. Like I said, just stopped by to wish you my best," Hanson said.

The colonel turned back to Blackwelder. His look wasn't unsympathetic, but it was stern, as hard as the steel girders that held the ship together. "Just finished reviewing your scores from our most recent arms training, Blackwelder. Exceptional. Can't wait to put that eye of yours to good use."

"Yes, sir."

Colonel Hanson gave Blackwelder a knowing nod and excused himself to the bar.

The three of them sank back into their chairs a bit uneasily. Blackwelder's latest run-in with the brass had left him shaken and a little pale. He downed the remainder of his drink.

Abernathy reached out and patted Blackwelder on the hand. "It's nothing, okay? Just like Staff Sergeant Nguyen, back when we were in boot camp. He's just blowing smoke."

"Still, maybe you should lay off the party planning for a while," Macke said. "I'm sure Lyta and her friend Jacobson can handle it."

"Don't be ridiculous," Blackwelder said without any confidence. "Lyta's been fantasizing about finding her perfect prince and getting married for as long as I've known her." Another quick look passed between Blackwelder and Macke, but Blackwelder pressed on. "You're one of my best friends. I want to be there for you."

"I'm your best friend!" She punched him in the arm from across the table. "I know you two like to think you're it, but you never would have even met if I hadn't introduced you. So I should get top billing."

"You absolutely should." Blackwelder's smile faltered. Macke and Abernathy acted as if they didn't notice. "Well, I'm gonna get going."

"Already?" Abernathy asked.

"Yeah, I'm on rifles tomorrow. And being hungover around the ammo, even the practice rounds, is a recipe for disaster. We can talk more about the party tomorrow, though. I promise."

"A word before you go?" After Blackwelder nodded his assent, Mack kissed Abernathy on the forehead. "Be right back, babe."

Macke followed Blackwelder back through the archway and onto the observation deck. Blackwelder didn't stop until he'd reached the lower deck, now empty and guaranteed to stay that way until after the 2030 booze rush died down.

Down on the level, the deck had a photograph taken at the peace accords, the summit where 75 percent of the world's leaders created the Allied Earth Council. In the photo, thirteen men and women shook hands as if they'd always been best friends. As if each of them hadn't tried, on more than one occasion, to blow the other up. Blackwelder focused on Chancellor Bumani, the former French president who, five years prior, had somehow managed to get everyone on the same page just in time to stop the Elumerians from blowing a gigantic crater into mainland China.

"What are you doing, Wellie?"

"Spencer," Blackwelder corrected.

Macke sighed. "Look, I know that Hanson sniffing around for a bite can really mess with your head, but you've got to keep your shit together around Lyta. She's been asking me what's wrong with you."

"What's wrong with me? What's wrong is that I've been living a fucking lie, Robby! I'm secretly in love with my best friend, not to mention fraternizing with an officer. With Lyta, I'm betraying the one person who's had my back since day one, and I'm hiding my true self from every other person on this boat. It's not fucking fair."

"Look, Spence, I really don't want to have this conversation with you again. It can't be the way you want it to be, okay? No matter how unfair it is. And it's unfair to all of us, not just you."

"I'm not talking about me, for once. I'm talking about Lyta. Every time I see her face I hate myself that much more. I'm sleeping with her fiancé while helping her to plan her engagement party. Do you have any idea how fucked that is?"

Blackwelder turned toward the view. From this angle, he caught a much better shot of Saturn's rings: hundreds of thousands of kilometers of ice and rocks and dust. He wondered if he'd ever see anything as beautiful again in his lifetime.

"I can't do it anymore," he said, turning back toward Macke.

"You're not going to tell her, are you?" Macke furrowed his brow, and his expression soured; an intense panic seemed to be coming over him. "You can't! Do you have any idea what that will do to her?"

"I know. But I can't keep lying to her either. That's why I'm leaving. I'm transferring to Triton, to the front line command at Fort Felix. I'll be leading their marksmanship training."

"You can't be serious. Triton? With all that second-rate colony tech? Every other day you hear about somebody getting nitrogen poisoning or freezing to death. And you heard what Lyta said: it'll most likely be the Elumerians' first target when they come back."

"I know. That's why they need trainers. I'm gonna stay on board the Barack until after this party, and then I'm gone."

Blackwelder started to leave, but Macke grabbed him by the arm.

"Wait. Just...wait, okay?" A deluge of emotions flushed Macke's face: anger, confusion, fear...love? Desperation. Blackwelder's own heart pained at the sight of him. He wanted to hold him, even started to open his arms, but remembered where they were and thought better.

"Don't," Blackwelder said. "Because there's nothing you can say—"

"I'll tell her. I swear. I just...I just need a little more time, but I promise." Macke started to shiver as if he'd walked into a cold front.

"No. If you don't love her, which I know you do, then don't marry her. But don't tell her because you're trying to convince me. It'll destroy her. And quite frankly, you deserve to carry that guilt and shame around. We both do."

"But you're throwing your life away." Macke's expression was strangely emotional, but his volume was quite controlled. "No one asks to get sent to Triton. The number of people who actually make it back—"

"It's my choice, Robby. The leadership sets the attitude of this place, and that's not going to change any time soon. You heard Hanson; it's only a matter of time before someone starts asking, and I have to start telling. At least this way, the two of you don't have to get implicated in any stupid scandal of mine. Besides, it's only a six-month tour. I'll be back before you know it." The lie was already effortless. Blackwelder knew he'd be saying it to himself every day until he met his end.

"Spencer...please...."

Blackwelder headed for the door again, but this time, Macke didn't try to stop him. For the briefest of moments, Blackwelder hoped that he would. But when the door closed behind him, he breathed a sigh of relief: he had survived the temptation. He'd passed the test. He'd proven that his head could rule his heart. As he made his way back to his quarters, though, he was unsurprised at how little comfort that fact actually brought him.

Chapter Three: Dawn at Fort Felix

BLACKWELDER BOARDED THE transport as quickly as possible. It was 0400 Standard Earth Time. He didn't want a send-off, and he certainly didn't want a scene. He knew Lyta would ask too many questions. Robby, he was less concerned about; he doubted Robby could come up with anything more convincing than what he'd already said, and there was no way he'd say any of it in front of other people. Still, a quiet exit was easier. Cleaner. Colonel Hanson had approved the request for the early departure without question. It was obvious he understood. So Blackwelder boarded the transport, strapped himself in, nodded to the pilot, and departed. He couldn't have known it for sure then—though of course he suspected—but he would never step foot onto the AES Barack again.

AFTER A LONG series of hyperspace jumps, Blackwelder's new home came into view. Triton was a bright white dot, shining at the edge of human space. They looked like handsome jewels together: Neptune, a giant sapphire, and its moon, a little pearl spinning happily around it in a perfectly circular orbit. They were beautiful, but he didn't want to think about that. Instead, he reminded myself that this is where it would happen. When they finally came back, when the war finally resumed, this would be where it started. The vaunted glory of the front line. As he approached Triton, more and more of the surface became visible. A pinkish band stretched across the southern pole of the moon. Unlike Earth, or even Neptune, Triton didn't have much atmosphere to speak of, and the pink mark looked like a scar on the skin of the world, like a trail a blood left on the snow-covered rock.

He should have been filled with dread. He should have been afraid, and yet, all Blackwelder could do was crane his neck like an excited child as the transport made its final descent toward the base. Triton's surface was covered in dazzling ice and snow, or at least what would pass for ice and snow, as water was actually very rare on the moon's surface. Crystals began to form along the edges of the window, confirming what he'd read about Triton only a day before: that its surface was actually colder than its atmosphere. They flew through a couple clouds of dark gray dust before finally spotting the base. It was a massive compound, broken down into multiple domed sections that were connected by several covered passageways, most only big enough for foot or small cart traffic, but the two biggest domes were connected by a large corridor that could easily accommodate a tank. The pilot tilted toward one of the large domes, and a small port opened up to reveal a hangar bay below. Even from that altitude, a small assemblage of women and men were visible in the dome. On the floor near where they were standing was the base's emblem: nine white stars arched and floating above a golden trident pressed again a blue shield. The tips of the trident and shield seemed to be pointing to the gathering in what felt like an obvious and intentional way. Apparently, he was going to have to endure a scene after all.

Once on the ground, the hatch to the transport slid open. Blackwelder stole a brief moment to adjust himself, to make sure his uniform was presentable. They'd been flying for twelve hours, and it was the first time he'd ever worn the new uniform, so he'd allowed himself to get at least a bit more comfortable by unbuttoning the jacket and loosening the tie during the trip. The last thing he wanted was for his new commanding officer's first impression of him to suggest he was in any way messy. Promotion or no, he was still the best-dressed enlisted man in the Allied Earth Force.

After exiting the transport, he came to attention before two women and two men. The person closest to the middle stepped forward and extended her hand.

"Warrant Officer Blackwelder, I am Lieutenant Colonel Andrea Lee, Area Commander for the Weapons Training Battalion, and your new Commanding Officer. Welcome to Fort Felix."

Lt. Col. Lee was a bit taller than Blackwelder. She had black hair that was white at the temples. It hung loose, as it was too short to be pulled into a ponytail. She had the kind of face that looked like it couldn't help but smile.

"Thank you, sir." He shook her hand. "I am very pleased to be here."

"This is my XO, Major Arthur Page," Lee said.

"Sir," he said, saluting the major. Page was very tall with a lean build and head full of white hair. Blackwelder couldn't help but think that Page was too old to only be a major. It was a centuries-old expectation that an active duty officer should continue to progress through the ranks, at least until the level of colonel or a similar position. A notion inspired, Blackwelder assumed, by sharks, one of the ocean's great predators, who had to keep moving forward or die. That Page had presumably been passed over for promotion to colonel or even lieutenant colonel seemed suspicious. Especially as promotions were easier to come by during a time of war, a fact to which Blackwelder could personally attest. But, perhaps Page had simply grown comfortable working with Lt. Col. Lee? He would not have been able to serve as her executive officer if he shared her rank or outranked her.

"Warrant Officer Blackwelder," Page said coolly. His stare gave Blackwelder the uncomfortable sensation of being probed, as if Page could somehow hear his judgmental thoughts. His facial expression didn't change at all, though. He reminded Blackwelder of men he'd seen during boot camp and basic training: men with something to prove but without all that reckless bravado. Presumably, he was incredibly well disciplined (as XOs should of course be) but probably held a grudge. Blackwelder suspected Page was the absolute last person he'd ever want to cross. He averted his eyes but held his salute until the colonel spoke again.

"And this is my SNCO Sergeant Major Vernita Burton."

"Warrant Officer," Burton said, saluting him. Her voice was sonorous and commanding, as though she had enough authority in one hand to lead all of the Allied Earth Forces.

Blackwelder returned the gesture. "Sergeant Major."

Vernita Burton had a presence that was hard to define. She was taller than average, but not distractingly so. She radiated a well-defined sense of control, like the XO, but there was also something infinitely more pleasant about her. Even from her stance, Blackwelder could tell that her physical training was superior, and that she was confident and capable. He had a feeling he was going to like her.

Lt. Col. Lee indicated the last man standing with the welcoming party. "And last but certainly not least, this is Fort Felix's senatorial ambassador, Mr. Juan Miguel Arías."

"Warrant Officer Blackwelder, on behalf of the Tridecagon of Allied Earth, I'd like to welcome you to Triton and Fort Felix. I understand your mission here will make us all much better prepared to move forward in this war," he said, shaking Blackwelder's hand enthusiastically.

Juan Miguel Arías. He had bronze skin with baby-soft hands, just like a civie. He had the practiced tone of a politician, but his amber eyes emoted sincerity. His black hair was short but wavy, and he smelled like...like a forest after a light rain. It had been years since Blackwelder had spent any time in the forests near his childhood home in the Allied Earth region of America North—his father's native Canada, to be specific—and yet here he was, somehow connecting to one of his favorite places from his youth. His head began to swim. Captured snapshots of Juan Miguel's smile started floating down the river of his thoughts. His name, Juan Miguel Arías, licked Blackwelder's ears like a song. He could feel Juan Miguel's heartbeat in his fingertips as they shook hands. It was the last thing he could have ever expected to find in Fort Felix, out of all the places in the universe; he had found him.

Blackwelder closed his eyes and opened them again. He was desperately hoping that he hadn't been staring at this man for the last ten minutes, that any of the thoughts he'd just been having hadn't accidentally slipped from his lips, in whole or in any part. Suddenly his mind returned to him. He had merely blinked. It had been seconds, not minutes. And he had managed to keep his mouth shut, both verbally and physically.

"Thank you, Ambassador. It's very nice to meet you." He pulled his hand from Juan Miguel's grasp. He took a step back and tried not to stare too intently at the floor. It was incredibly childish, he knew, but he just couldn't bring himself to look Juan Miguel in the eye.

"Well," Lt. Col. Lee began, cutting in, "I'm sure you're a bit tired from your travels. I will see you in my office at 0800 tomorrow morning. In the meantime, I will leave you in the sergeant major's capable hands."

"Thank you, sir." And with that, Lt. Col. Lee, Major Page, and the ambassador all turned to leave.

"Would you like to go to your quarters, sir?" Burton asked.

With great effort, Blackwelder finally tore his eyes away from the exiting welcome party. "No. The Training Grounds. Please."

"Very well. Corporal, take the warrant officer's belongings to the officers' quarters in C-Dome."

"Yes, sir!" A green-uniformed blur sped past off to the transport. Blackwelder nodded to the soldier as he collected his bags. Burton indicated a cart parked nearby, and following her lead, he jumped in the passenger side.

They left the hangar in D-Dome and entered B-Dome, which was sometimes referred to as the central hub because from there, one could access any part of the base directly, except for the officer quarters, engineering, and the brig. On that first day, though, they drove through B-Dome in silence. Blackwelder pretended to be carefully observing the structural work of the walls and ceilings, such as the crisscrossing white beams, and the spotless sheets of thermo-glass, the only thing standing between them and temperatures one hundred times colder than the Arctic Circle back on Earth. Every time they passed a fresh-faced enlisted private, they saluted him. He had only officially become an officer about twenty-four hours prior, the gold bar and single red star on his collar still as new to him as he was to everyone else. Whether Colonel Hanson had convinced Admiral Vaughn to authorize the promotion out of a sense of respect, or as a celebratory "good riddance," he guess he'd never know.

But really, it was all just a distraction from what he was really thinking about: Juan Miguel. And almost immediately, he began to feel guilty. What about Robby? Was he somehow betraying him by moving on so quickly and completely? In every way that mattered, he was the reason Blackwelder had even decided to come to Fort Felix, why he couldn't continue the life and career he'd begun aboard the Allied Earth Ship Barack. And who was to say that he was actually moving on? There were no guarantees there; he and Juan Miguel had barely exchanged names. He was convinced Juan Miguel was gay, though; his "q-th sense" was exceptional and had never once failed him. But even with that, Blackwelder realized there was no reason why an ambassador to the Allied Earth senate should take even the slightest interest in him. And what if he were another closet case, like Robby? He didn't think he could stand to go through that again. Why was he even still thinking about Robby? He was literally billions of miles away, most likely getting married to his other best friend.

"Sir," Burton said, "we've arrived at J-Dome, the Training Grounds."

Realizing that their cart had come to a stop, he quickly pulled his thoughts back in line. "After you, Sergeant Major."

Burton punched a code into the keypad, and the doors slid open. As they walked inside, lights on the floor illuminated a path inside the chamber, where several more pathways became apparent. They proceeded down the walkway, the lights on the ceiling activated, casting a bright but pale blue hue across the chamber. The intersecting white beams climbed their way up one wall and down another, and from the center of the room, he could look straight up through the thermo-glass into the Triton sky outside, which was practically no different than staring directly into space. This room was incredibly clean, almost sterile, as if he could eat off the floor. He could tell the custodial detail must have worked very hard to keep a base so big looking like that. In fact, the place seemed to be in better condition than the Barack. He was beginning to wonder where all the fuss about the "deadly colonies" had come from.

In the heart of the room, where the other paths intersected, there was a platform with a console. Burton stepped onto it and began fidgeting with one of the keyboards. A holographic image projected from the panel in place of a monitor, but then it disappeared just as quickly. Burton scowled at the console, jabbing her thick fingers at it a couple of times before giving the whole unit a swift kick. Finally, the screen reappeared. There, perhaps, was some of that infamous reputation at work.

"To the left are the weight room, combat training, and the obstacle courses. To your right is the small arms locker. And the infirmary. The locker only contains practice weapons; no live ammunition is stored here or allowed in J-Dome. The infirmary is only equipped to handle minor incidents. Anything more serious than a bruise or minor bleeding should be treated at the hospital, in M-Dome. There have been very few minor injuries; either the men just walk it off, or they literally can't walk. That infirmary is probably the most boring detail on the whole base."

The image of an entire troop of soldiers limping out of the training dome sprang up in Blackwelder's mind, their shoulders badly sprained or their socks filling with blood, each too proud to be the first one to have his or her "minor" injury taken care of.

"Straight ahead, you'll find the shooting range, the arms obstacle courses, and the instructional classroom spaces. Your office is next door to the classrooms and across from Second Lieutenant Greene."

"My office," he scoffed. "Hit a target enough times in a row, and apparently they'll give you a commission. Or at least a warrant."

"We're at war, sir. And from what I've heard, you're a man with a talent. Talents are highly prized just now."

"I suppose."

"Have you done much instructing before?"

"Only unofficially. Only my squad. I was a better shot than my lieutenant, so he always let me set the example. What's that dome over there?" He pointed to a blacked-out dome closely connected to the one they were in.

"We call it the Arena." Burton stroked the touch screen, and a corridor connecting the two domes lit up. "You're aware that the 'daily' rotation of Triton takes 5.9 Earth days, sir?"

"Yes," I said, having only learned that fact shortly before arriving. Burton smiled; apparently he'd passed the test.

"Despite this fact, we still operate under Earth Standard Time. The sun being visible or not will rarely correspond with the supposed time of day. Not unlike life on a ship in Saturn space, as you were, but as the 'days' are even longer here, it will take some getting used to."

"I bet."

"The Arena is designed to be our ultimate combat simulator. Once a training group enters, no one can get in or out for one Tritonian day."

"A six-day training exercise?"

"It's not just six days. It's also under Triton-norm conditions. Or at least partially. That means cold suits and oxygen masks."

"That seems a little over the top."

"Real battles are rarely fought on schedule. Sir. And every person on this base needs to be prepared for the day real battle comes to Triton."

There was that tone again, that voice that could bring an entire army to a standstill. Blackwelder felt pitied under her gaze. He was in danger of losing whatever cred he had earned by doing his homework.

"Of course, Sergeant Major. You're right. I look forward to completing the Arena myself. I'll obviously need to if I'm going to train others under those conditions."

Burton gave him a subtle nod. ."Have you seen battle, Sergeant Major?"

Burton hesitated. "Yes. The Battle of the Crescent Moon. I was part of the first squadron of Marines—back when we still had Marines—sent to engage the enemy on the Moon. They called us 'Combat Astronauts.'"

"You were a Dead-Naut?" he said, hardly able to contain himself.

"Yes, some people called us that, too."

In that moment, he had never been more attracted to a woman before. Burton's flawless skin was a deep dark brown, which reminded him of his Kenyan grandmother's, and as far as he could tell, she wore very little makeup, save for a thin line of eyeliner and just a touch of pale pink lipstick on her bottom lip. She wore a traditionally military haircut, a close-cropped low fade, and her imperious cheekbones seemed to promise destruction to lesser facial features belonging to anyone else that dared to challenge them. To be sure, he wasn't at all confused about his sexuality, but Vernita Burton could not be denied; she was a goddess. A beautiful, deadly war goddess.

"I'm sorry, I don't mean to gush. It's just that you are the reason I enlisted. I was sixteen when the Elumerians attacked out of nowhere, and was just about to start tertiary school. Half my freshman class was threatening to drop out and enlist. They actually had to send recruiters to our school to tell us *not* to sign up. Well, everyone except for me. I wasn't sure if the military would be the right...fit. I finished 14th grade and actually enrolled in art school. You know, good hand-eye coordination and all. I'd won a couple competitions here and there as a kid, and I couldn't think of anything else to do, so I figured I'd give it a shot. But then I saw that documentary they did on you all, the first humans to battle an alien race. The stories of how you all kicked alien ass on the moon before the cowards went and blew half of it to dust...you and your team basically made the Allied Earth possible. I enlisted the next day."

"Crescent Moon was a massacre," Burton said without meeting his eye. "We were completely, hilariously, unprepared. The only saving grace was that the Elumerians seemed to be equally disadvantaged. We floated and bumbled around in the dark like children, a lucky shot here, a fortunate stab there. Aliens and humans killing our own as often as we got the enemy. When they finally dropped Cradle Maker, it was obvious they were trying to salvage the situation, save at least a little face. Very few beings walked away from that battle. I was extraordinarily lucky."

Burton returned her attention to the console. She busied her hands, though he wasn't sure if she was actually doing anything.

"I'm sorry. I had no idea."

"The command staff is aware of my record, obviously, but I would appreciate it, sir, if you didn't share this with anyone else. Time wasted treating me like a hero is time better spent preparing to fight."

"Of course, Sergeant Major. You have my word."

Blackwelder joined Burton on the central platform but kept his distance. He accessed another touch screen from the secondary console port. The system was similar to the one used on the Barack but different enough that it would take some time for him to learn to fully navigate it.

"Can you show me the most direct route from here to my quarters? I imagine this will end up being my first destination in the morning and my last stop at night."

"Of course." She crossed the platform to stand beside him. With a few keystrokes, she brought up a map of the base. "As you see here, most domes connect to B-Dome, the central hub. But instead of going all the way over to B, it will be much faster for you to cut through the hospital in M-Dome to get to C-Dome. Officer quarters are there on the middeck."

"Perfect. Thank you."

"The command staff quarters are on the upper deck of C-Dome. The general, the area commanders, and the other upper-level officers. The ambassador is a civilian, though, so his quarters are in I-Dome."

Blackwelder froze. Had he given himself away? Was this the confirmation? He was not prepared to alienate himself on his first day on assignment.

"Permission to speak freely, sir?"

"Of course, Sergeant Major. You don't ever need to ask," though he was already starting to regret those words.

"You should talk to him."

"I—what?" he managed, looking for the nearest exit.

"Ambassador Arías. He seems like a good man. I haven't had many personal interactions with him, but he's well respected on base. Very few ambassadors live in residence, and the ones that do tend to be lazy wastes of space. But this one earns his keep. The general usually sends him to handle anything that comes up with the civies. He's sort of their de facto CO. And he runs interference with the Tridecagon whenever possible, so the general can stick to the actual work of running a military base at war."

"That's great that he's so, um, great. But I don't know what we would need to talk about." Blackwelder hoped his deflection was convincing. He busied himself pretending to inspect the other buttons on the console.

Burton came around to face him. "If you're worried about command, don't be. Lieutenant Colonel Lee is a big old romantic when it comes to these things. And the general cares exactly zero about anyone's personal life. Again, base at war. The only person who would even say anything is Major Page, and as long as you don't let it get in the way of work, even he'll be cool."

He gave her a pathetic, incredulous look. She put her hand on his shoulder. "You're not on the Barack anymore."

"Thank you," he said, finally beginning to feel like he wasn't being set up. She was right. He was at Fort Felix on Triton now. He had come all that way to move on from the mistakes of his past; he could at least try to put that ship behind him, even if he knew to do so honestly may take a little time.

"Call me Burton," she said as she headed back toward the entrance.

"Thanks, Burton."

"You're welcome. Care to follow me to the Cave? You look like you could use a drink."

"Thank you, but I'll pass this time. I think I'll keep taking a look around, check out my office."

"Then I'll leave you to it."

"Two sessions in, and I can already see improvement," Captain Albermarle said. "I can hardly believe it. You're quite the teacher."

Blackwelder blushed hard. "Bossa Squad is a talented group of soldiers, sir. It's got nothing to do with me." Blackwelder flicked the air, causing the holoscreen to scroll as he continued to review the most recent training scores from Albermarle's personal squad.

"Your style's a little unorthodox; I would never have thought of having them square off against holographic projections of themselves, and Greene certainly wouldn't have come up with that. But I can't argue with results."

"It just seemed to me in our very first session that your squad was obsessed with beating each other. Very motivating, for sure, but ultimately stagnating, after you become one of the best squads on the base. This way, their true opponent is themselves, and they can always be better."

Albermarle tapped the screen projection a couple of times, adding checkmarks to his document before swiping his finger across a blank field, which automatically added his signature. "Well, like I said, you can't argue results. Which I'm sure has Greene all twisted up in knots."

Blackwelder looked up from his screen. "I'd like to think my presence here frees the second lieutenant up from having to run the marksmanship courses so he can really focus on combat training. It's a team effort here in the Weapons Training Battalion."

"Hmph. Not only can he shoot, but he can dodge too." Albermarle chuckled to himself as stepped off the platform. "But that will serve you well, I think. Greene can be... difficult. Interest you in a drink? I'm meeting up with some folks over at the Deck."

"No, thank you," Blackwelder said, returning his attention to his screen.

Albermarle headed toward to the exit doors. "Suit yourself."

"Sir, before you go?" Blackwelder tapped his screen with two fingers, then dragged the image to the end of the console before flicking his fingers in Albermarle's direction. Albermarle's wrist lit up as his personal com device activated, revealing the screen Blackwelder has been reviewing. "Can you tell me anything about his group?"

Albermarle expanded the screen and scrolled for a moment. "Ah. Brant Squad. Toward the bottom of the totem pole, really. I haven't dealt too much with them."

"It looks like they don't have a regular squad leader either?"

"If I remember correctly, they had someone when they were first formed, but he was transferred off the base inside of a month. They've been leaderless ever since. Why? You thinking about taking them on?"

Blackwelder scoffed. "No, of course not. I was just wondering why they're performing so poorly. I should probably keep an eye out for them."

Just then, the doors to J-Dome slid open. Major Page strode in, causing Blackwelder and Albermarle to snap to attention. Following just behind him though was Juan Miguel. Blackwelder caught sight of him and almost forgot he was mid salute. The ambassador's dress shirt was unbuttoned to his mid chest, and his sleeves were rolled up. He looked like he had just stepped out of a rerun of one of those old legal shows Blackwelder used to watch as a kid. Blackwelder found the look quite alluring.

"At ease, gentlemen."

"Major Page, I was just complimenting Blackwelder on Bossa Squad's marked improvement after only a couple sessions."

"Yes. Well I am sure Lieutenant Colonel Lee is quite pleased. I found this one on my way," Page said, pointing nonchalantly toward Juan Miguel.

Juan Miguel extended his hand to shake with Page, then lightly patted him on the back. "You were right, Major; Captain Albermarle was here. Thanks for the chat." And then, to Albermarle, "You ready to go?"

"Yes. Blackwelder, sure you don't want to join us at the Deck? Final call."

Blackwelder smiled slightly. He wanted to blush, but he was mentally willing the blood to abandon his cheeks. "Thanks, um... but no. I think I'll pass."

"Then we shall depart," Albermarle said. He left J-Dome with Juan Miguel close in tow. Before he exited though, Juan Miguel turned back to Blackwelder and gave him a slight nod and a wave. Was it Blackwelder's imagination, or did he seem disappointed?

Page walked over to the console and activated a view screen. He casually glanced at several screens with his eyes narrowed, a sign, Blackwelder was sure, that meant his work was being closely scrutinized. He didn't take offense to it. Blackwelder was, after all, new to this base. He had a lot to prove, and there was no telling what Hanson had shared ahead of his transfer. Impressing Page seemed like it would be the hardest thing to do in his new situation, so naturally it became Blackwelder's top priority.

"It does look like Albermarle's squad is seeing some minor improvement. Nothing to get too excited about."

Though no longer at attention, Blackwelder remained still with his hands clasped behind his back. "Yes, sir. It's only seventeen percent for the squad overall. But individually, some squad members have seen improvement upwards of twenty two percent. And, to be frank, sir, each additional shot made is another Elumerian dead."

Page smirked. A small crack in his icy exterior. "Indeed. Now if we could apply that efficiency to all of our enemies...."

"The Retribution, sir?"

Page straightened and turned to Blackwelder. He had fallen back into the impassive expression he wore when Blackwelder first met him, making him very difficult to gauge. "Allied Earth's most dangerous terrorist organization. What's your take on them?"

Blackwelder frowned. "My take, sir?"

"Yes, your opinion."

Blackwelder was confused. He understood the question, of course; he just didn't understand why he was being asked it. "Well, they've got a rising death count. They've mostly attacked government installations, but I don't think that means civilians are safe. I'm not exactly sure what their grudge is, but being active at a time like this threatens the existence of the entire human race."

Page paced the platform. His heavy footsteps echoed off the high ceilings. Still, that look of calm. Blackwelder found it quite unnerving. "Officially, they're anti-government. They want to see Allied Earth crumble. But some would just describe them as a bunch of old, mostly white men still fighting the tidal wave of change and decrying the loss of privilege. That's a very naïve view though; they seem quite adept at convincing younger men to fight and die for them."

"Young or old, I think they all need to be decisively dealt with, sir. We should be doing everything we can to ensure they no longer pose any level of threat."

"Good lad," Page said, turning on his heel. His whole demeanor seemed to change once his line of questioning had ended. "I look forward to seeing more of your progress," he said as he exited J-Dome.

Blackwelder stood in stunned silence for a few moments after Page's departure. He was certain his interrogation had been a sort of loyalty test, and fortunately, he had passed. Were the Retribution a threat to them, even that far away from Earth? Honestly, he hadn't spared them too much thought since shifting his entire life into the depths of space, but as he returned to his work, Blackwelder thought that he'd best keep his eyes open.

Chapter Four: The Cave

"GOOD WORK TODAY, Bonner," Blackwelder said. He stood beside the door as the hard-light simulation deactivated, returning what had been a grueling three-dimensional firearms obstacle course to a largely empty blue-gray chamber. Bonner grunted as she walked by, too tired to form real words. One by one, his students exited the obstacle course, most of whom were likely heading to the mess hall.

"You're definitely improving, Chiu," Blackwelder said. "Do those exercises I taught you." Several more students filed past him, each looking more beleaguered than the last.

"Sir," one of the soldiers said quietly, "I would have totally had that last run if it weren't for Petrey. He's holding us all back!"

"You're a team, De Silva," Blackwelder said. "You've got to learn to work together. If you don't all make it, none of you do."

Dissatisfied with the response, the soldier began to walk away.

"If it makes you feel any better, though, I can assure you that you were nowhere near nailing that last run, even removing Petrey as a factor. See? You can all work on improving together."

De Silva opened his mouth as if he wanted to say something in response but apparently thought better of it and begrudgingly took his leave.

Once they'd all left, another man walked over, the gold bar with its single silver star on his lapel turning a greenish color in the blue hues of J-Dome. A coincidence, as the name stitched underneath the bar was also Greene.

"Maybe we need to keep an eye on that one," Greene said.

"De Silva, sir? He'll be all right. He's actually got the makings of a decent leader, if he could just stop focusing on himself for five minutes." Blackwelder let the door to the obstacle course chamber slide closed behind him as he made his way back to the console in the center for the dome. From there, he brought up the controls for the practice dome and began to reconfigure them.

"You worked them pretty hard today," Greene said.

"Brant Squad is the lowest performing group on base, Lieutenant. They need the extra push."

"True. I'm just not sure they're worth the effort."

"Every single soldier on this base needs to be able to pull their own weight, sir. God forbid we're in the middle of an attack or some freak accident occurs, and Brant Squad ends up the only group left still able to fire a weapon. All of Allied Earth will be glad someone made the extra effort with them."

"All right, all right. No need to break out the International Anthem on me," Greene said. "Do what you like; everyone figures you're the boss in J-Dome anyway."

Blackwelder smirked as he continued to enter commands on the touch screen.

"So when are you gonna meet me in the combat circle? A little hand-to-hand training?" Greene asked.

"Right after you accept my invitation to do the marksmanship run. In the meantime, I'm going to run a norm-grav simulation. In case anyone's looking for me."

"Suit yourself. We'll be at the Deck, if that interests you at all," Greene said as he turned to exit. Blackwelder watched him leave, not the least bit saddened by his departure.

Blackwelder entered a few more sequences into the computer until a digitized voice said, "Triton-Normal Gravity Firearms Exercise, activated." A path illuminated from the platform to the simulator doorway, where he'd just dismissed his class. A green light flicked on to the right of the door.

He walked over to the small arms locker. Inside the locked chamber was an assortment of handguns and small automatic rifles. There were some that fired lasers, some that discharged energy bursts, and some that still fired traditional bullets, though all the weapons in J-Dome were equipped with non-lethal practice rounds only. All except the gun in the steel-gray locker in the back of chamber marked "Blackwelder." He opened the locker and retrieved the L9L14, a laser pistol based on the design of the M9 pistol United States military personnel started using in the late 20th century.

Though he was an expert with most firearms, this pistol had felt right to him from the first moment he'd held one in basic training. The barrel was seven inches long, and the grip panel and safety fit his hand as if it had been molded just for him. Some people reported being distracted by the way light sometimes reflected off the barrel's silver finish, but that had never bothered Blackwelder. If anything, it helped him focus. He flipped the magazine release, which unlocked a red-striped energy pack from the base of the gun. He might have been one of the only people allowed to carry live ammo into J-Dome, but there was no reason to waste good fire power on a training run. Instead, he inserted a blue-striped energy cartridge and flipped another switch near the pistol's barrel. He listened for the characteristic zip-click sound that meant the cartridge had been accepted and that the gun was powered and ready. With that, he headed for the practice chamber.

Blackwelder had been on the Barack long enough to master simulated Earth-norm gravity and zero-gravity, but he knew he needed to better familiarize himself with Triton's relatively light gravity if he were going to successfully lead a group through the Arena. Six days in training with a group like Brant Squad; he cringed at the thought.

The door to the simulation chamber slid closed behind him with a heavy thud, and he was in total darkness for a moment. It was always his favorite moment, right before an exercise engaged; in the silence, all he could hear was his heartbeat, and the hairs on the back of his neck stood up as the blood rushed to his head. The external sensory deprivation mixed with the anticipation gave him an unmatched high.

The moment passed, and the lights came back up. Immediately he felt the weightless sensation pass over him. His feet were still on the ground, but he knew that just by flexing his big toe he could propel himself into the air.

"Commencing Triton-Normal Gravity Firearms Exercise," the computer said. Holographic red rings of varying width and clustered like bull's-eyes began to materialize around the room as small gun turrets rose from the floor and descended from the ceiling.

The game was on. Blackwelder shunted to the right to avoid a blast, then quickly returned a single shot to eliminate the bull's-eye. Though the strike counted, it clipped the target, and almost didn't connect at all.

I slid too far. I'll better compensate next time.

He ran forward and tucked into a front flip to avoid the next barrage (in which he was able to complete three full rotations thanks to the lax gravity), stuck his landing, and took out three bull's-eyes in a row. He smiled. Blackwelder wasn't a boastful man, but he was very good at what he did. As people sometimes pointed out.

BLACKWELDER STOOD AT the bar, waiting for the chance to place his order. He tapped his fingers on the metal surface, not out of impatience, but more from a nervous energy he could only attribute to his surroundings. The Cave gave him mixed feelings. On the Barack, the 2030 had always felt easy, simple; like sort of an equalizer on the ship. On Triton, though, things were different. At once, more open and accepting, and yet still exclusive. Blackwelder still felt a bit on the outside, but how much of that was his own fault? How much of that was him still clinging to places and faces he'd been so familiar with before?

The bar tender appeared in front of him. She wrung her hands with a towel and gave him an expectant nod.

"Two vodka ceelos, please."

The bartender nodded again and got to work preparing his drinks. As he watched her though, the sound of his name drifted across his consciousness. Blackwelder was a fairly distinct name, so he was certain that when he heard it, he was being referenced. He looked over his shoulder to see a group of soldiers huddled together. He assumed they were trying to be inconspicuous with their gaze, but they were failing. He recognized them as members of Brant Squad, who he had been paying more and more attention to lately. As Brant Squad failed yet again to be subtle as they all looked away from him, the bartender returned with this his drinks. The pale neon green liquid had an other-wordly quality, but its cheap price and high alcohol content made it a staple in Blackwelder's repertoire. Activating his touch-com, he tapped it a couple of times to pay the bartender, and then took the drinks back to his seat.

Burton reached for the drink as Blackwelder approached the table. She took a sip, staring over the rim of the glass at the Brant Squad members a few tables away. "Admit it: the reason why you come to the Cave instead of the Deck with the other officers is so you can hear this lot ooh and ahh over you."

"That is definitely not why I come here." Blackwelder considered it for a moment. "I suppose it doesn't hurt, though."

"You should probably spend more time at the Deck. People might start to question it. Second Lieutenant Greene, for one."

"Second Lieutenant Greene is kind of a Malfoy, don't you think? Besides, you outrank most of them in spirit. I'll hang out at the Deck when they let you hang out at the Deck."

"In spirit, maybe," she said, "but not in metal." She tapped her insignia, a black chevron with three stripes underneath it. "Still, I could go to the Deck right now, and I doubt anyone would say a word about it. But what would be the point? I like it here."

The Cave was a wide room filled with white tables and chairs and enlisteds and civilians alike tired from a long day's work. The center row of lights had shorted ages ago, creating a shadowy aisle down the middle of the room. The regulars said they liked the effect, so the general had called off the repairs. In one of the corners, the base bookie had set up a board with all the open bets. People could place odds on everything from what tomorrow night's dessert would be to when and where the next fatal equipment malfunction would take place.

Blackwelder took another sip of his drink. "I like it here too."

Burton rolled her eyes. "No, you don't. You're just avoiding the Deck because that's where the ambassador hangs out."

Blackwelder choked on his drink. "What? No! Of course not. That has nothing to do with it."

"Right. Just ask him out already. I definitely would, if it were an option."

Blackwelder sat his drink down. He knit his fingers together, stared at them for a moment, then futilely pulled them apart again. "It's more complicated than that."

"It's only as complicated as you make it."

"Well, if it's so simple, what about you?"

Burton smiled as she brought the drink back up to her lips. "I have someone. Nothing serious."

"Really? Who?"

"Sergeant Wyatt. In Engineering."

"Engineering...the scrawny redhead? That guy?"

"You like what you like," Burton said, finishing off her drink. "Besides, that man has skills." She put her glass upside down on the table and got up. "You could spend the rest of your time at Felix ducking around corners, trying to avoid him, or you could just pull the trigger. Aren't you supposed to be a good shot?"

BACK IN THE practice chamber, Blackwelder aimed the laser pistol over his shoulder. He exhaled for a fraction of a second, shifted his weight to his left heel, and squeezed the trigger. A blue light shot from the gun and hit the last bull's-eye dead center.

"Triton-Normal Gravity Firearms Exercise, complete. Training score: 100 percent," the computer said.

Blackwelder sighed. He was a good shot. It was time out for the insecurity.

Blackwelder arrived in E-Dome and began making his way to the Deck. He was on a mission, barely acknowledging the few familiar faces he passed along the way. He arrived at the entrance to the bar, but then stopped. He wanted to walk in, but his legs had locked, rooting him to the spot. Panic rising in his chest, he looked wildly to the left and the right before his eyes landed on an image of Fort Felix's emblem imprinted outside the bar. Seeing the stars gave him a strange sense of comfort. There was one for each of the Solara-Neuf, even Pluto, which had been downgraded and upgraded to and from full planet status at least half a dozen times before the United Nations finally decided to permanently upgrade the planetoid when they built an observatory there. It was an amusing bit of trivia that had completely distracted Blackwelder from his mission, until he saw the ambassador exiting the bar.

"Ambassador Arías," Blackwelder stammered.

"Oh, Warrant Officer Blackwelder. Nice to see you again," Juan Miguel said, extending his hand.

"You too, sir. Are you heading to the Deck?"

"No, just leaving."

"Right. Obviously, sir."

"Please, call me Juan Miguel. I'm just a civilian; I don't really go for the whole rank and title thing."

"That's easy to say when your title puts you on a level with the general."

"I suppose it is," said Juan Miguel. His smile made Blackwelder feel empowered and a little reckless. "Well, goodnight, Warrant Off—"

"Would you like to get a drink with me?" Blackwelder blurted out. "Not tonight, but hopefully soon."

Juan Miguel's eyes widened at the question, but he smiled broadly as his face quickly settled into a pleasant expression. "I...sure."

"Great! We could maybe meet here tomorrow or something."

"The Cave would be fine, too. If you wanted. I know you like to hang out there."

"You do?" Blackwelder asked. The ambassador blushed. Had Juan Miguel been asking around about him? "On second thought, let's make it dinner. And you can call me Spencer."

"I'd like that a lot. See you tomorrow night, Spencer."

Juan Miguel turned to leave, and it was only at then that Blackwelder realized that their handshake had never broken, that they were still holding hands.

BLACKWELDER SAT ACROSS from Juan Miguel, trying to look everywhere except at his date. He'd been filled with a terrible excitement all day long; Burton had even made fun of him for knocking over a couple of corporals in his rush to leave J-Dome. He had agonized over what to wear, but seeing as how he only had one collared shirt outside of his uniform, the choice was made for him. He even arrived at the commissary fifteen minutes early to try and eek out the best spot for them: visible from the entrance, so he could see Juan Miguel arrive, but not too visible. He didn't want them to be on display. He had played out multiple conversations in his mind, saw himself laughing effortlessly with the handsome ambassador sitting across from him. But now that he was actually in the chair, his mind had gone blank.

Juan Miguel took a sip of his drink, then dabbed his chin with his napkin. He had an air of etiquette that Blackwelder couldn't help but admire. "So, how are you adjusting to Fort Felix?"

"I'm good. It's good. It's going good. Well," Blackwelder stammered. He deflated a little in his chair and took a long gulp of his drink. The door fell into his line of sight, and it took a concerted mental effort not to make a run for it then and there.

Juan Miguel, however, didn't seem to notice. "You've been active duty for some years now. Ever miss civilian life?"

"Civilian life? You mean like before I signed up for the chance to die any day now fighting aliens?"

They laughed together at the remark. Blackwelder could feel the knot in his chest loosen. His attention was drawn to Juan Miguel though, whose laugh, deep, sincere, and just the tiniest bit naughty, reverberated through his body. The science of the twenty second century had brought mankind many things that they had previously consigned to fantasy, but sitting across from Juan Miguel, Blackwelder found himself believing in magic. As the laughter subsided, Blackwelder looked down at his plate. He felt nostalgia rising up inside him, and he wanted to filter himself, be careful with his words.

"I do miss my mom's cooking. She baked. She could put anything into a pie and make it taste like a dream. In the winters, she would make this pot roast pot pie that was so good it would make you cry."

"Actual tears?"

Blackwelder looked up. He dared to stare back into those amber eyes. Juan Miguel was beautiful, and it somehow felt appropriate to think of his face while also thinking of home. "Sure. Actual tears." Blackwelder smiled broadly.

Juan Miguel reached across the table. He caressed Blackwelder's fingers with his own, and intertwined them together. "Well, I hope to see you as happy as your mom's cooking makes you, but at the same time, I hope to never see you cry."

Blackwelder was speechless again, but this time he wasn't upset about it. There has been so much space between them before, but in that moment, it was as if they couldn't be closer. Blackwelder thought that it might be quite nice to sit in this comfortable silence for the rest of his life. At the very least, it wouldn't be a problem for the rest of the night.

Chapter Five: Brant Squad

"I'M SURE YOU'VE noticed this, sir, but they're kind of kicking our asses," Chiu said. He panted heavily as he wiped sweat from his brow.

"They're not even advancing on our position anymore," Bonner said. "They're just playing with us."

Blackwelder could feel the exhaustion coming off each member of Brant Squad. They'd been "playing" a war game, Melee Combat, against Greene and Wilder Squad, and it had not been going well for them. Each team started out with a certain amount of territory—lime-green boxes illuminated on the ground of the simulator—and the goal was to protect your boxes, your territory, through armed and unarmed combat in each section. Hits equaled points, and anyone who received a certain number of points was considered "dead" and had to sit out until the next round.

In the beginning, Wilder Squad had taken it easy on them. The match-ups were clearly one-sided; on average, Greene's soldiers were five to six inches taller and 20-plus pounds heavier, but both sides seemed to be giving out similar numbers of points. Wilder won the first two rounds with only a couple of their team members still active. After that, though, they started competing in earnest. They wiped out all of Brant Squad without taking a single point for themselves, and then pressed on, which allowed them to take three more boxes in rapid succession, forcing Brant Squad to keep reentering the fight without being able to take a rest. Now, with only one box left, they'd finally granted Brant Squad a short reprieve.

"I just want this to be over already," Bailey said. The others were clearly in agreement.

Blackwelder's thoughts ran in conflicting directions. He agreed with them, of course: they were clearly outmatched by Wilder Squad, and no amount of positive reinforcement was going to suddenly push them into the lead. From his side of the combat field, Greene sneered. The squad commanders themselves weren't allowed to engage in the combat, for better or worse, which left Blackwelder completely unable to pull out some last minute trick to save his team. On the other hand, it also prevented him from trading blows with Greene directly, which Blackwelder knew would have made his rival all too happy. Despite this, though, Blackwelder knew he couldn't simply let his team walk away defeated. The blow to their morale would be devastating, and he wasn't entirely confident that he'd be able to bring them back around.

"So it's obvious we aren't going to 'win' this exercise," Blackwelder began, thinking fast, "but I still want you to walk away having learned something. Today's lesson isn't about defeat, but about teamwork. We rise as a team, and we fall as team. If you go back out there only worried about your points and focused only on your opponent, this will be over in an instant. But if you work together, set your collective sites on a shared goal, maybe you can still claim a small victory."

They all looked at each other with blank stares. For a moment, Blackwelder wondered if his last-ditch effort would fall flat, but then Petrey began nodding his head.

"One shared goal," Petrey said. "We're going to lose. There's no doubt about that at this point. But, we don't have to be *shut out*. They haven't taken a single hit from us in the last three rounds. Let's get in one good hit before this is over. And let's make it count!"

The squad huddled together and plotted. Blackwelder started to join them but thought better of it. They were inspired, and he wanted this victory, however they would attempt it, to be wholly their own. He couldn't help but overhear mention of the name Kiosev, though. Kiosev was the biggest, scariest guy on Wilder Squad. He was hauntingly pale with cold eyes and a mirthless smile, and over the course of the exercise, he had personally eliminated each member of Brant Squad at least once. Blackwelder's crew had set their sights right for the top.

At the sound of a chime, the final round began. Instead of moving to take on each of their opponents individually, though, Brant Squad broke into two groups: Bonner and Chiu dropped to the ground and laid down cover fire while Petrey, Bailey, and De Silva tore straight up the middle toward Kiosev. Seemingly stunned at their audacity, Kiosev left himself open for a moment too long, which was all the time they needed. Propped and propelled by Bailey and De Silva on either side, Petrey ran full speed and launched himself into a backflip flash kick that caught Kiosev squarely on the jaw. He was lifted a couple inches off the ground before he came crashing back down.

Wilder Squad's vengeance was swift. Mere moments later, they had mercilessly dispatched every member of Brant Squad and won the exercise. But the damage was done; Kiosev, who hadn't taken a single point the entire game, was out cold.

The simulator doors slid open and Major Page appeared. "Looks like our winner today is Wilder Squad. Though you may want to get him checked out," he said in Greene's direction.

Ten minutes later, after the squads had cleared out, Blackwelder stood at the center console, reviewing footage from the exercise. He was interrupted when Greene stormed up to him.

"What the hell was that?"

"To what are you referring?" Blackwelder said calmly. He glanced over at Page, who was also still standing on the central platform. Greene was possibly angry enough to attack him, but Blackwelder wondered if he'd risk it right in front of their XO.

"That fucking stunt back there! Kiosev's chin had to be stitched up!"

"Sorry if my squad got a little rough with your guys," Blackwelder said, trying not to laugh.

"Don't give me that! We destroyed you out there. And then your worthless space monkeys foul our best man, like the sorry excuses they are!"

"Look, Greene, you won the exercise. They got in one good hit. Just one. Are you really telling me your entire squad's ego is that fragile?"

"You know damn well that if I had turned all of Wilder loose on one member of your squad, you'd be screaming bloody murder right now!"

"Yes, probably because your Neanderthals would have actually killed someone!"

"Enough. The two of you, bickering like children. It's unbecoming," Page said. "There were valuable lessons all around: humility in victory, victory in defeat, and two of the most important rules of combat—never let your guard down, and never underestimate your opponent."

"But sir—" Greene began, but he was interrupted by an urgent beeping on the console.

"This is Postmaster Zeng with an all-points wave out of Mediterrasia: a military factory was bombed today in the city of Cairo. Sixteen dead, fifty-seven more injured. The Retribution is claiming responsibility. More as it develops."

"Those bastards," Greene spat.

"I know we're fighting a bigger enemy, but the Tridecagon needs to devote more resources to bringing these terrorists to justice," said Blackwelder.

"The only justice for the Retribution is a bullet to the brain," Greene said. "In fact, I'd kill each one of them with my bare hands, if I could."

Blackwelder shook his head. "From zero to murder. Why am I not surprised?"

"And what? You're supposed to be sympathetic? They just killed sixteen people. Two months ago, it was nine people in Indiopacifica. These wastes of human space are out to destroy us and our way of life, but I'm guessing you think we should be showing them some kind of mercy."

"No, definitely not mercy, but the answer isn't whole-sale slaughter either. We should understand them better and deconstruct their rhetoric. Otherwise, they'll just keep winning new people to their twisted cause. Like the Elumerians; they didn't just get up one day and decide to cross half a billion light-years because they hated our way of life. They have a reason for wanting us dead, too, I'm sure."

"I can't with you," Greene said. "You're weak, your squad's weak, and if you don't get your shit together, you'll all probably end up as target practice for your precious Retribution. Or the Elumerians. Or both." He stormed out of J-Dome without another word.

"Someone's got a hard-on for the Retribution," Page said coolly.

Blackwelder turned to face the major. "I'm sure he thinks he's being patriotic."

"I'm sure. Except, how does that old saying go? Something about protesting too much? Makes one wonder... Anyway, that was quite the show out there today."

"Yes, sir. I'm proud that they were able to eke out a small..."

"It was pathetic. It would be funny, if it weren't so damn tragic. Your squad was destroyed, no two ways about it. If this had been real combat, if actual human lives had been on the line, then God help us all."

Blackwelder stiffened into attention, bracing himself for impact.

"Brant was already one of the lowest performing groups before you got here, so that can't be attributed to your nascent leadership, but still, I expect better."

Blackwelder's breath held until Page finally exited J-Dome. The major's words echoed through his mind. He would need to find a way to help Brant Squad improve, and quickly. Sure, he'd been a part of some high-performing squads, especially Jinx, but he'd grown up with that group, really, even though he was their sergeant. He hadn't *built* them. If Blackwelder was going to achieve that now, he knew he'd need help.

"READ 'EM AND weep, ladies," Burton said. She dropped her hand of cards to the table deliberately, for dramatic effect. When they landed, they revealed a straight flush. The other four women at the table threw down their cards in exasperation. With a wide grin, Burton raked the folded pieces of paper from the center pot toward her. Every week, Burton challenged some of the other female enlisted officers to several hands of poker, and most nights—certainly not all, but most—she came away the victor. They didn't gamble for money, but instead for favors, chores, and privileges, which made Vernita Burton one of the most well-connected people at Fort Felix.

"Well, the night's still young. Shall we go again?" Burton began. She glanced around the table but, in doing so, spotted Blackwelder approaching. "Or perhaps not."

She normally thought of Blackwelder as being more assured when he entered a room, but instead he seemed strangely fidgety. "I apologize for interrupting your game, ladies. Burton, could I please have a word?"

Burton glanced around the table half expecting someone to object, but was met with what appeared to be unbothered expessions. She stood. "They're secretly grateful. I was about to *really* ruin their nights."

In what would pass for a quiet spot in the Cave, Burton got the rundown from Blackwelder of Brant Squad's abysmal training performance and Page's soft threat.

"I know you don't typically assist with training individual squads, but I could certainly use the help."

"They're good kids. They just need a little extra attention."

"I'm willing to give it to them. But we could all use a little guidance."

Burton thought to herself for a moment. Something interesting was bubbling up. "I have an idea."

She walked back over to the table, where another game had started in her absence.

"Fakhoury, your team's monitoring the water systems tonight, right?" Burton asked.

"Yeah," she said.

"I need a favor." She handed Fakhoury one of the folded pieces of paper from her winnings that night.

A couple hours later, Burton had devised a scheme she was pretty proud of. Blackwelder was right, in that she rarely did training on this level anymore. Not since her days of fighting live battles and being more directly responsible for the lives around her. If she was being honest, though, she missed that excitement, that rush of adrenaline that came from suiting up and firing her weapon with abandon. She didn't miss seeing her comrades dying, of course, but with war you had to take the good with the bad. And Blackwelder was a good kid. A friend. It had been interesting watching his mind work, watching him navigate Fort Felix in the short time he'd been there. He reminded her a little of herself, too, which also made her more willing to help.

It was 0300 Earth Standard Time, and the members of Brant Squad were sound asleep in their barracks in F-Dome. She liked messing with them while they were asleep. No better way to test and stress constant readiness. The squads were formed around living quarters, so the five or six people assigned to a shared living space often comprised the majority if not the entirety of a specific squad. The quarters were T-shaped, with a small foyer at the entrance, two bathrooms off to either side, and a long narrow space where the beds were lined up against the walls across from each other. Aside from a few uncomfortable-looking desks, each person had a wardrobe and a foot locker, which constituted the entirety of this living space.

Suddenly, the sprinkler system activated at full power, blasting ice-cold water down onto the unsuspecting squad. Shocked cries were choked out between involuntary gulps of water as each member in turn spilled from their bed.

Once they'd all stumbled into the center of the room, looking dangerously wide-eyed, Burton nodded to Blackwelder.

"Fall in!"

At his command, Brant Squad immediately snapped to attention, though several of them shivered and squirmed as the cold water continued to pelt them. Slowly, the water ceased, and Blackwelder and Burton came fully into the room, still perfectly dry. Blackwelder stepped forward.

"We all know how Melee Combat went against Wilder, so none of us should be surprised that we're standing here. We've got a lot of training to do, and it starts right now."

Brant Squad really was the worst of the worst. Admittedly, she didn't originally understand why Blackwelder had taken such an interest, and indeed, why he was inching ever closer to officially taking them on as his own squad. But as he was pleading his case to her earlier that evening, she thought of Crescent Moon. She wondered how many of her fellow soldiers' lives would have been spared if someone had taken Blackwelder's level of concern in seeing them properly trained and prepared.

She looked at the assembled squad members, pathetically soaked and shivering, and yet, there was a real determination in their eyes. That, she could work with. "Now that I have your attention," she said, "we can begin."

Chapter Six: The Arena

"LET'S GET THIS over with," Major Page said. Arms folded, the XO shook his head as he surveyed the team. Brant Squad stood at attention, though their expressions betrayed a severe nervousness. The situation was made worse by the presence of Greene and his Wilder Squad. There was no doubt that they had come to gloat, belittle, and intimidate Brant Squad, but the XO's presence had curtailed their baser instincts. Instead, they were left sneering on the sidelines, Kiosev looking particularly murderous.

The XO's gaze fell on Blackwelder.

"At ease, Warrant Officer. All of you," Page said. "Should I be expecting more of what I saw the last time I observed your training?"

"Brant Squad's been working very hard since then, sir," Blackwelder said. "I'm sure they...we will perform admirably."

Page grunted, then turned to Greene.

"Still, a little competition never hurt. Might help push all involved to a higher level of performance. How about it, Greene?"

"Wilder Squad plays for keeps when we train, sir," Greene said with an adolescent grin. "The real bad guys use live fire, and so do we—safety protocols off. I'm not sure the warrant officer and his...squad...are up to that sort of challenge." Several bystanders chortled at the remark. Blackwelder shot Greene a dark glare.

"Sir, it's highly irregular from what I've been told for more than one squad to enter the Arena at a time. And training without the safety protocols engaged—"

"Relax, son. I was only making a joke. As I'm sure Greene here was as well. We are all aware of how dangerous the Arena would be without fully functioning safety protocols."

For a moment, Blackwelder felt like the nerdy kid in class who corrects the teacher. Greene rolled his eyes, driving the point home.

"And you," Page said, turning to Burton. "What in the Solara-Neuf possessed you to volunteer for this little excursion?"

"My trigger finger was feeling itchy, sir," Burton said. "Figured this would be the best way to get some relief before the real thing shows up."

"Well it's not the normal order of things. I'm still amazed the lieutenant colonel approved it. Speaking of—" Page was cut short as Lieutenant Colonel Lee and Juan Miguel entered J-Dome.

"Atten-hut!" shouted Page. Everyone in the room snapped to attention.

"At ease," Lt. Col. Lee said. She walked over to Brant Squad and called each soldier by name—Petrey, Chiu, De Silva, Bonner, and Bailey—as she inspected their uniforms. They were dressed all in white, from their skullcaps to their boots. Their parkas, unzipped, revealed reinforced plating on their jackets that, already a grayer shade of white, shimmered like silver in J-Dome's lighting. Large packs hung from their backs like mischievous primates. Bonner, the shortest member of the unit, swayed slightly as the lieutenant colonel approached her, but she quickly corrected her posture and stood firm. She gave her a little wink as she passed on. Standing before the entrance, located between the small arms locker and the infirmary, the white of Brant Squad stood in stark contrast to the blacked-out Arena silhouette looming behind them.

"I came to wish you luck today, Warrant Officer Blackwelder. Heading into the Arena after only seven weeks on base. I believe that's some sort of record, no?" Lt. Col. Lee said. She turned to Page, who grunted in the affirmative and gave a stiff nod. "Well, you do the entire Weapons Training Battalion proud by your enthusiasm and ambition. I expect your mission will be a complete success." She scanned Brant Squad one last time. For an instant, she seemed if she might withdraw that statement, but the moment passed, and she bathed them all in a confident smile.

"I just wanted to wish you luck too," Juan Miguel said, guiding Blackwelder off to the side. "Not that you'll need it, I'm sure." Juan Miguel patted Blackwelder once on the shoulder and gently passed his hand down Blackwelder's arm.

"Preparation's far more reliable than luck," Blackwelder said awkwardly, as if he were about to follow his statement up with a sharp sniff and a move to adjust his glasses. Recovering, he added, "But I'd be a fool to underestimate either." He gripped Juan Miguel's arm at the elbow. He let Juan Miguel's amber gaze transfix him, and for just a moment, he contemplated leaning in and kissing him right there. A quick glance at Major Page broke the spell, though. Page cocked an eyebrow at Blackwelder, which was all he needed to remember himself. He squeezed Juan Miguel's arm again and rejoined Brant Squad.

"One hundred forty hours, ladies and gentlemen. Second Lieutenant Greene will watch the clock and monitor your vitals," Page said.

"Brant Squad, sync touch-coms on my mark," Burton said. Each member of the squad slid their fingers down their forearm to activate their personal view screens. "Ready...mark!" They tapped the screens in unison.

"See you in six days, Lieutenant Colonel, Major. Ambassador..." Blackwelder said. The two senior officers nodded. Juan Miguel smiled warmly.

The doors to the Arena slid open. Blackwelder turned his back so that he faced Brant Squad with the assemblage behind him, but he spoke loudly enough to be overheard.

"Brant Squad, remember your training, and remember what we're up against. Everything in there is a hard-light holographic projection, but that doesn't mean it won't walk and talk and smell and sound exactly like the real thing. Now, there are those who would doubt your ability, your dedication, maybe even your right to be here. But I've seen you. Each of you. You've worked hard for your place here, and I'm sure you will show all of Fort Felix why it should be proud to count you among its ranks. Let's get it done."

Blackwelder marched his company into the dark tunnel, and the doors slammed shut behind him with several ominous clicks and the flash of a red light. Blackwelder's turn in the Arena had officially begun.

REMAINING: 134 HOURS

Brant Squad marched silently through flat white terrain. The sun, however faint in the sky, reflected harshly off the snow-covered ground. De Silva walked twenty paces ahead of the group, while Bonner brought up the rear, struggling under the weight of her pack. Fatigue showed on each soldier's face, except for Sergeant Major Burton, whose easy gait and blank expression belied the physicality of the procession.

"We've been at this for hours," whined Petrey. "Can we stop for a break?"

"You don't stop until the squad leader says so!" shouted De Silva over his back.

Blackwelder and Burton exchanged quick glances. He considered the drooping shoulders and the slowing pace of the squad. "This is as much an exercise in endurance as anything else, but yes, we can take a brief break. Five minutes."

"Five minutes!" De Silva said, marking the time on his touch-com.

The soldiers dropped to the ground where they were standing, immediately reaching into their packs for water. Burton took a quick pull from her water bottle, then returned it to her pack.

He watched her for a moment, noticing a barely concealed smile. "You seem to be enjoying yourself."

The smile deepened. "I am. The familiar burn in my thighs, some hard-earned sweat, a little fresh air...or what passes for it, anyway—"

"If even that. The air seems...off." He activated his touch-com.

"You smell something?"

"Well, no. But I'm getting a feeling." He looked at his view screen. "The O-2 levels are a little lower than I'd like, but they're within norms. Of course, if there were a nitrogen buildup in the atmosphere, we wouldn't know it until it was too late. Gotta love those odorless gasses."

"I'll sync my com with the J-Dome monitors. If the air balance has any critical shifts, we'll know about it."

"Thanks. Greene will probably catch any fluctuations before we do, but it's always good to have a second pair of eyes on. This group certainly doesn't need anything else to worry about—what's that?" In the distance, a low whistling sounded, like something moving through the air. Fast.

Burton looked up, surprise etched across her face. "It's a manta flyer!"

"Incoming!" Blackwelder screamed.

A small black vessel shaped like a stingray appeared on the horizon and blazed toward their position. Three bright white lines illuminated across the nose of the ship just before a barrage of blue laser fire peppered the ground. Barely having time to get back to their feet, the squad dove in all directions as the blasts cut a neat path right down the middle of where they'd been resting. The ship then banked hard, preparing to come back for another run.

Blackwelder waved his arms dramatically, trying to pull everyone toward him. "Form up! We need to take cover!"

"Cover! Where? We're in the middle of nowhere," Bailey said.

"The holo-cage in your pack, Bailey. Good for detaining captured Elumerians, yes?" Blackwelder pulled several pieces of machinery from his own pack.

"Yes, sir."

"Why?"

"Because of the high-density force field. It guards against projectiles, laser fire... Oh! On it, sir!"

"Bonner, Chiu, help him out. Petrey, De Silva, Burton, on me. Suppressing fire. Knock that thing out of the sky."

De Silva sniggered. "Not likely with Petrey's aim, sir." He lined up the sight on his weapon.

"Just get it done!" Blackwelder said.

Petrey, De Silva, and Burton opened fire, sending blue laser bursts into the air from their rifles. Bonner, Chiu, and Bailey quickly staked four telescoping poles around their position. As the ship made its second pass, several shots came across the craft's nose, while one blast had direct contact with one of the wings.

Petrey threw his hands up excitedly. "I hit it! Did you see that? I hit it!"

"Keep firing!" said Burton.

"Oh right. Yes, sir!" Petrey immediately returned to his task.

The squad's blasts knocked the ship off course by a couple degrees, causing its return fire to miss the heart of the assemblage, but not clear them entirely. Bonner caught a powerful shot in the back, burying her face-first in the snow.

"Bonner!" Bailey cried.

"Activate the cage, Bailey! Now!" Blackwelder said. He barely looked up from his own project, the large weapon he'd been assembling. "The rest of you, hold your fire!"

The shooting came to an abrupt end as Bailey flipped a switch on one of the poles. They extended seven feet into the air. At their apex, the poles were connected by an electric current that ran down all four sides. The ship fired again, but the cage halted its attack. The poles vibrated menacingly with the force of the blasts, but they held.

The ship came around, preparing for its third pass. Having completed his handheld rocket launcher, Blackwelder stepped outside the confines of the cage. He hoisted the launcher onto his shoulder and sank down onto one knee. He took a deep breath.

The enemy ship sped toward them. Blackwelder held fast.

"What are you waiting for, sir?" demanded De Silva.

"The whites of their eyes," Blackwelder whispered to himself. Just as the spark of white began to streak across the enemy craft, Blackwelder squeezed the trigger. The launcher fired; a bright-blue explosion thundered above them as two distinct halves of a ship soared over their heads and plummeted like fire balls to the ground somewhere in the distant horizon.

"Pit stop's over," Burton said. "I suggest we find some real cover."

Blackwelder strapped the weapon to his back. "Agreed. Bonner, are you alright?"

Dazed, Bonner pulled herself out of the snow. Her forehead was bruised from where she'd made impact with the ground, but otherwise, she seemed unharmed.

"Yes, sir. I'm fine."

"No, you're not. You're dead. Maybe next time for real. Watch your back."

"Yes...sir," said Bonner.

REMAINING: 105 HOURS

De Silva, Bailey, and the other squad members huddled around a geyser in the frozen crust of Triton's surface while Blackwelder quickly finished a scan of their supplies. Curls of thick, dark, odorous smoke rose into the air, but there was no heat.

De Silva waved his hand in front of his face. "Ugh, Jesus, Petrey! What did you eat?"

"Leave him be, De Silva," Blackwelder said. "You know it's not him."

"Yes, sir. I was just joking with him, sir."

"It's the methane from the geyser!" Petrey said.

"They're called cryovolcanoes," Bailey responded. "They literally shoot ice instead of lava. They're kind of amazing."

"They're kind of everywhere," Chiu noted. Indeed, Brant Squad had chosen to take their break in a field of cryovolcanoes. The natural formations lined up along deep cracks in the ice.

"I had no idea," said Bonner.

De Silva tapped his temple knowingly. "That's cuz they keep what goes on in here pretty tightly under wraps. Callo Squad was the last group to do the run, so I asked them what it was like. They wouldn't tell me anything, but Duke's eyebrows haven't been right since!" They all shared a laugh.

"It's good that you're paying attention to the terrain," Blackwelder said. "It's not just the Elumerians we're up against in here, but the landscape itself. I wouldn't be surprised if one of these things erupted."

Bailey and De Silva exchanged mischievous looks.

"Get some rest while you can."

Blackwelder turned and made his way over to Burton, who had posted up a good distance away.

"What are those monkeys up to?" Burton asked.

"Nothing good, I'm sure," Blackwelder said. "And why do you call them monkeys? I heard Greene say something like it once too."

"It's just the name we give to newbies here at Felix. Every base does things a little differently."

"Yeah. On the Barack, we called ours 'dusties.' You know, like space dust?"

Burton stared blankly at him.

"Yeah, I suppose monkey has a bit more punch to it."

"So as I was saying, before you suddenly needed to do a pack check: how are things going with the ambassador?"

"Oh. That," Blackwelder said, as an unmistakable grin crawled across his face.

"Yes, that. Don't try to play with me."

"We've been on a few—some—dates," Blackwelder said. "He's, I don't know...he's kind of great. Which seems weird, right? He's a politician, with powerful connections to the Tridecagon. One would assume. And yet, he seems so normal."

"Well, the civilian staff love him," Burton said. "He knows them all by name, asks about their families, the whole deal. The brother of one of the cooks died recently, and she couldn't afford the trip back to Earth for the funeral, so the ambassador paid for the ticket out of his own pocket."

"Oh great. So you're telling me he's a saint."

"No such thing, sadly. He's affable, but he's got secrets. I can see it in his eyes. But I think he could be good for you. You could be good for each other."

"Maybe after I discover his big, dark secret, we can all double-date, you and Wyatt."

"Wyatt and I do all of our dating behind closed doors, thank you. I have no use for the gossip and speculation."

"That attitude just feeds the speculation," Blackwelder said. "Half the base thinks you're a lesbian."

"Let 'em think what they want. It doesn't stop me from getting mine.".

Blackwelder pulled his water bottle from his pack. "I'll drink to that." They cheered each other and took long pulls from their bottles. As Blackwelder returned his water bottle, counting began in the distance.

"What are they—" he began.

"Go go go!" Bailey shouted.

The five young soldiers ran and dove to safety just as a massive fireball erupted above the geyser.

"All right, pack it in! Break time's over! Let's get a move on," Blackwelder said. Then, more softly, "Before you kill yourselves."

REMAINING: 89 HOURS

Sec. Lt. Greene walked up to the monitor on the main console in J-Dome. The faint beeping of vital signs echoed off the polished floors and high ceilings. Brant Squad appeared to be in relatively good health. Some were clearly more anxious than others, but they were all alive. Greene tapped the screen that displayed the ratio of the elements in the air. The nitrogen was a little high, but nothing to worry about. The temperature had dropped a few degrees since his last inspection twelve hours ago, but as the normal temperature was already so far below livable, that hardly seemed to matter. He next passed in front of a video screen that showed Blackwelder and his troop huddling inside a cave-like structure.

Greene hmphed at the scene. "Yeah, just spend the next ninety hours in your little hole and call it a day." Satisfied with himself, he left J-Dome.

INSIDE THE ARENA, Brant Squad had come across an impact crater whose walls had crumbled over time, creating a small pocket just big enough for the seven of them. It was dark now; what little light the sun spared for Triton had disappeared and was replaced by the blackness of space. In the depths of the cave, the squad sat around a device with lots of cylindrical markings that hummed loudly. Each of their suits was connected to the small metal box, drawing power. Their normal uniforms now carried the addition of a glass-fronted helmet.

"It's freezing in here," Petrey said, rubbing his gloved hands together. "And this helmet makes me claustrophobic."

"Well, you could always just take it off," De Silva said. "At -235° C, I figure both of your problems will be solved in a matter of seconds."

Bailey, Chiu, and Bonner all laughed. Petrey just quietly hung his head.

"In all seriousness, though, it is pretty cold in these things. My suit's only registering about 8° C," Chiu said.

"Yeah, is that normal?" Bonner asked.

"This is as much an exercise in—" Blackwelder began.

"—endurance, etc. etc. Yes, we know...sir," De Silva added quickly, noticing Blackwelder's expression.

"You already know that every twelve hours, the atmosphere will toggle between Earth-norm and Triton-norm. Which means we're going to get plenty of experience in trying not to freeze to death. Just keep your suits connected to the faichauder. It'll keep you warm so your suits don't have to draw on internal power."

Everyone nodded and fell silent again. Bailey pressed his back against the curving wall of the cave and drowsily closed his eyes. The others tried to follow suit. Blackwelder exchanged a concerned look with Burton, who also showed a moment of alarm. Despite this, he too closed his eyes and fell into a light, uneasy sleep.

Four hours later, Brant Squad was already up, packed, and on the move again. They'd stowed their helmets, as the temperature controls had reactivated, and had covered several miles in the faint, distant starlight.

De Silva passed his binoculars to Blackwelder. "Sir, up ahead,"

Approaching on the horizon, the wreckage of the flyer he'd shot down earlier lay in two blackened, ruined halves.

"We'll scout the ship, check for survivors. Weapons live," Blackwelder commanded, and the zip-click of energy cartridges let him know his order had been carried out.

They cautiously entered the crash site, weapons drawn. The two burned-out husks looked like the charred remains of a massive land mammal, as if it were the starting point for some sort of mechanical elephant graveyard.

"Chiu, get a closer look at their systems. Bailey, cover him," Blackwelder said.

"Sir." Chiu and Bailey moved away from the others.

Blackwelder pointed at De Silva. "De Silva, defensive positions."

"Sir." At once, he pointed out positions for Bonner and Petrey so that the three of them created a perimeter between the two portions of wrecked ship.

After completing his inspection, Chiu walked back over to Blackwelder. "Most of the systems appear to be fried, sir. The fire melted these consoles clean through."

"Okay. Anything else?"

"There are three sets of controls, three operable stations on what's left of the main deck. But there are no bodies, sir."

"Maybe they evaporated in the fire?"

"They're alive," Burton said suddenly. "Watch your backs!"

But before anyone could heed her advice, a hail of blue laser fire threw the scene into chaos, catching Bonner in the chest, clipping Bailey in the shoulder, and sending the rest of Brant Squad clamoring for cover behind the two halves of busted ship.

"Return fire!"

"Light 'em up!" Burton added.

Blue blasts criss-crossed through the air as Brant Squad fired in the direction of a ridge a couple hundred feet away. The ridge was the outer edge of another impact crater, one that had concealed the Elumerians' presence. Bonner, winded but not incapacitated, crawled to cover beside her fellow soldiers, while Blackwelder began to reassemble the launcher.

After a few minutes of exchanging fire, Burton turned to Blackwelder. "This is pointless. We're too well blocked by the ship, and they are perfectly concealed in that crater. But neither of us can move. We're pinned down."

"I know. Hold your fire!" Blackwelder said. "This baby's our best shot, but at this distance, it's...imprecise. I can hit the ridge, take down some of their cover, but there's no telling how deep that crater is. Even without the extra cover, they may still have the ability to hide, and we still won't be able to approach without fully exposing ourselves."

Burton tapped her weapon against her pack. "Note to self: next time, pack the grenades."

"Sir, we can cobble together a few flashers," Chiu yelled from behind the other half of the wreckage. "The explosive yield might not be that high, but combined with the noise and the light discharge, it should be enough to drive them out of the hole."

"Do it," Blackwelder said.

"Yes, sir! I just need to get my—" Chiu began, but as he spoke, he stepped from behind the edge of the ship for just a moment. Sparks flew as red laser blasts dead-ended against the wreckage. A well-aimed shot found Chiu's leg, though, and pierced his thigh. His white suit and the snow behind him was splashed with red, and Chiu crumpled to the ground.

"What the hell just happened?" De Silva said. "He's bleeding!"

Burton shook her head. "But that shouldn't be possible, not with the safety protocols engaged."

Indeed, the very point of safety protocols was to prevent a situation like that from occurring. Blackwelder was horrified at the thought that the hard-light projections they were up against were suddenly able to use live ammunition. Holographic enemy combatants made tangible by an error in a line of code... maybe the space colonies would be the death of him after all. Shelving that thought, his mind then turned to Greene, remembering his "joke" about only training with live rounds, and how Brant Squad wouldn't be up to the challenge. If he found out Greene had anything to do with this....

Though his thoughts were reeling, Blackwelder managed to keep his face impassive. Malfunction or no, every simulation had an end point. He knew if he could get them there, they'd all be fine. "It looks like the rules of what's possible and what's not just changed. Bonner!"

"Yes, sir!" She immediately dropped down to Chiu's side and started pulling medical supplies from her pack to attend to his wounds.

"We've got to end this now. We're all sitting ducks here, and they don't even have lethal rounds," he said.

"I do. Never leave home without one," Burton said.

Blackwelder smirked. "Neither do I. Chiu, are you alive?"

"Yes, sir," he called out weakly.

"Can you still make me that flasher bomb?"

"Yes, sir."

"Get to it, then. Sergeant Major? Let's do some damage."

"Yes, sir!"

Burton reached into her pack and pulled out a red-striped laser cartridge and loaded it into the magazine slot on her rifle. Blackwelder did the same, loading the lethal rounds into his silver-barreled L9. Bonner kept working on Chiu's leg while Chiu, on his back, continued to fasten the flashers together as the others handed them to him.

Careful to maintain their cover, Burton and Blackwelder opened fire on the Elumerians. Blackwelder's shots, though carefully aimed, were wasted on the perimeter of the ridge, as it provided perfect cover. His and Burton's return fire did slow the Elumerians' attack, though it didn't halt it altogether. And just as it had against the ruined ship's hull, the red laser fire sent sparks flying off the ridge, despite the fact that it should have been composed entirely of ice.

"Why is it doing that?" Bailey asked as he reloaded his rifle. "Is there a metal undercarriage in the crater or something?"

"No, the live ammo interferes with the hard-light projections," Burton said. She took her shot at a partially exposed enemy but missed.

"Normally, the simulator will compensate, but too much live fire can permanently damage the system. That's the reason we don't let you all practice in here with lethal rounds," Blackwelder said.

"Well, that, and so you don't kill each other," Burton added.

"Right. And with all the live fire we've already exchanged, there's no telling what harm's been done. Which is why we need to finish this now. Chiu?"

"I've got it, sir!" Chiu handed the improvised grenade over to De Silva, who tried to hand it to Blackwelder.

"Toss it," Blackwelder said, stowing his L9 and reaching for the launcher.

"Sir?"

"Toss the damn flasher, soldier! Over the ridge and into the crater, please. And now!"

For a moment, it seemed as if he wouldn't take the shot. As if, for all his bravado, he might actually let the pressure and fear of failure get the best of him. His gaze then fell on Chiu's injured leg.

"Yes, sir!" De Silva said. He reached back and lobbed the flasher high into the air. All of Brant Squad watched with bated breath as the flasher slowly descended toward its target. It landed on the edge of the ridge, but as luck would have it, it fell into the crater, and detonated a moment later.

The Elumerians let out surprised, guttural screams as they abandoned their hideout. A bright, yellowish light lit up the horizon as the ridge was leveled. The aliens were now defenseless. Realizing their position, the three Elumerians proudly got back to their feet. They stood seven feet tall on two long legs. Their shoulders were very wide, giving them incredible wingspans. They wore black exosuits with markings along the sleeves and across the chest that the humans didn't understand, but that Blackwelder had seen once before. The suits did not conceal the fact that their hands were webbed, their gloves resembling ribbed seashells. Under more normal circumstances, the aliens would have worn helmets, but as they were only simulations, Brant Squad was able to see them unmasked: they had pale, purplish skin and large bulbous, iridescent eyes. The gills up and down their neck slowly flapped open and closed. There was a nobility to these creatures, a beauty, matched by the intense hatred as all three let out a vicious war cry.

At once, they charged at Brant Squad, firing their red lasers from weapons similar to those Brand Squad possessed. Blackwelder hoisted up the launcher and sank down on one knee again. With the enemy lined up in his sights, he took his shot. A moment later, the three Elumerians disintegrated in a flash of blue light, their threat finally extinguished.

Bonner continued to work on Chiu's leg. De Silva stood, staring into the space the three aliens previously occupied. Bailey held his weapon, though his gaze was fixed on the ground, and Petrey, still crouching at the edge of the wreckage, stared imploringly at Burton, who now stood at Blackwelder's side. All of Brant Squad was silent as the smell of burnt ozone from the flashers wafted over the scene.

"So. Those are the aliens," De Silva said.

"I've seen the pictures, but never thought..." Petrey said.

"What were they saying?" asked Bailey. "It sounded like 'drunk scar.'"

"Obviously, it's their alien language," De Silva said, rolling his eyes.

Bailey scratched at this head. "No, it definitely sounded like English. Like 'funks tar,' or...or—"

"Junk Star," Burton said. "We thought we heard them say that too, when we fought face to face on the Moon."

"Junk Star...why does that sound familiar?" Blackwelder asked Burton.

"It was the name of that Astro-Command project from several years ago. That one that helped us get rid of all our trash before we buried ourselves in it."

Bailey snapped his fingers. "The Junk Star, I remember that. We had a kick-ass launch party for it!"

"Oh, right, that thing. But why would the aliens..." But his thoughts trailed to subjects too dark to speak out loud. "No matter. Our objective now is to get out of the Arena before anything else—"

But before he could say, the alarm on Burton's touch-com started blaring. "Sir, the oxygen levels are approaching critical. It's like the Arena is forcing another Triton-norm cycle,"

"But that can't be right! We shouldn't have one of those for another six-plus hours. The faichauder's not fully recharged yet from that last time!" De Silva said.

Blackwelder checked his own touch-com and had his suspicions confirmed; in less than an hour, they'd all be asphyxiated, frozen solid, or both.

"Helmets on, everyone. Looks like we'll be exiting the Arena ahead of schedule," Blackwelder said.

"Sir, what about Chiu? He can't walk on this leg," Bonner said.

"I'm fine, sir." Chiu tried to stand but when he did so, he crumpled back to the ground in obvious pain.

"He's not fine, and his suit's punctured! I've used the chem sealant to patch it up, but it won't hold for long against Triton-norm conditions."

"Dammit. Emergency shutdown it is, then. Blackwelder to J-Dome, Blackwelder to J-Dome: we have an extreme emergency on our hands. Request immediate shutdown of the simulation."

But there was no response.

"Come in, Second Lieutenant Greene, this is Brant Squad. Requesting immediate Arena simulation termination. Do you read?" But again, he was met with silence.

"There must be a short in the communications array," Burton said.

"Of course there is." Blackwelder typed furiously on his touch-com.

"But we'll be okay, right? Isn't there supposed to be someone monitoring us at all times?" asked Petrey.

"If there were, they would have shut this down when the safety protocols went off-line." Blackwelder then turned to Burton. "I can't raise the lieutenant colonel or the XO, and my emergency override codes aren't being accepted either. The receiver must have shorted; no signals are getting out of the Arena."

"Which means we'll have to patch in manually. But with the simulation still running, it will be difficult to find the control station."

"Well, then I'd better get going."

Burton nodded, and Blackwelder started running.

He ran as fast as his legs would let him, over the flat white expansive terrain, every few minutes looking to his touch-com to make sure he was heading toward the control station. As he feared, the atmosphere was gradually transitioning, the air composition shifting and the temperature beginning to drop. His suit would insulate him for a brief time, protect his squad for the moment, but De Silva had been right: the faichauder, a brilliant piece of self-charging technology, took hours to refuel itself. Without it, he knew their suits wouldn't be able to maintain warm enough temperatures. And Chiu...they'd patched his leg as best they could, but Blackwelder knew the chem sealant wouldn't hold. Their only hope was for someone on the outside to completely kill the simulation, returning the Arena to its blank, dormant state. A state not designed to kill his squad.

Fifteen minutes later, his touch-com began to beep, indicating that he was closing in on his target. His lungs burned with the effort, his head swam, and the blood rushed through him. He doubled over, but only for a few seconds as he took in huge gulps of air, gulps that chipped away at his own oxygen reserves. He pulled his L9 and, following the guidance on his screen, fired directly ahead of him. Instead of red lasers flying through the air, they collided with an invisible panel. Sparks flew as a ripple in the air revealed a translucent circuit breaker feeding a dark gray console. Blackwelder fired again, blasting the locked panel, which swung open to reveal a keypad, a screen, and some data ports. Moving quickly, Blackwelder plugged his touch-com into the control station and hammered away at the keypad.

"Emergency override rejected. Safety protocols contingency enacted," the computer said.

As Blackwelder had feared, the computer wouldn't allow the Arena doors to reopen as long as the safety protocols were disengaged. There'd be nothing stopping computer-generated Elumerians from walking outside and blasting every human they came across. Sure, they wouldn't last for very long, the farther they moved away from their source, but they could still do a lot of damage in that time.

"Send recorded message, secure channel: Lieutenant Colonel Lee. Sir, this is Warrant Officer Blackwelder. The Arena has undergone a catastrophic malfunction. My team and I are in imminent danger. I am attempting to manually override the system to force an emergency termination. Please assist."

The computer chirped, letting him know his message was being delivered.

Blackwelder slipped his fingers behind the screen and pulled several wires into his field of vision. He yanked the wires free at one end and began to twist them back together as he entered different sequences on the keypad. And then, he stopped.

"Send recorded message, secure channel: Ambassador Arías. Juan Miguel, it's me, Spencer. We've run into a bit of an...issue here at the Arena." Blackwelder went back to task, reworking the wires and trying to force the computer to accept his command. "We should be fine. I think I can get us out. I hope. Never done this before! But, in case I can't, I just wanted you to know—"

An electric shock ripped from the console, blasting Blackwelder backward to the ground. He lay in the snow face up as a thin wisp of smoke rose from his still, prone body, his last thoughts and unspoken words tumbling headlong into the darkness.

Chapter Seven: Testosterone

BLACKWELDER'S SENSES CAME rushing back to him at gale-force speeds. He shot straight up, eyes wide, his ears ringing. Falling back on his training, he started taking inventory of his surroundings: he was wearing a pale green robe and lying in a bed. He was not restrained. The walls were white and bare. The room smelled of tetrox, a powerful disinfecting agent, but normally the odor bothered him more, made his nose itch. They only used tetrox in one dome at Fort Felix, so it was safe to assume he was somewhere in M-Dome, in a hospital room. And he was shaking off a heavy sedative, or trying to at least.

Blackwelder began to relax. As he did, a voice called out to him. The most important detail in this room, and he'd missed it: he wasn't alone. He looked to his left; Juan Miguel came into focus, the worry pressed upon his expression somehow making him even more attractive. Blackwelder collapsed back onto the hospital bed.

"You're all right, Spencer," Juan Miguel said, rushing to take Blackwelder's hand. "Just take it easy."

As he stared at Juan Miguel, Blackwelder felt a rush of warmth come over him. It hadn't been very long, but he knew he was already starting to feel something for Juan Miguel, something he hadn't thought he'd ever feel again, really, much less so quickly. They locked fingers, and the warmth intensified. But it wasn't coming from their hands; the feeling spread through Blackwelder's entire body, as if the very thought of Juan Miguel had transformed into a bright light, shining in the darkness.

Blackwelder seized up. His body felt uncomfortably hot. He wasn't having an emotional reaction at all, but indeed a physical one, and something was very wrong.

"Spencer? Spencer!"

Blackwelder arched his back painfully. He locked his jaw involuntarily and was unable to speak.

"Jesus, you're burning up! Nurse!"

An alarm sounded and a woman in pale green scrubs rushed into the room, followed by another woman in a lab coat of the same color. The two women went immediately to Blackwelder's bedside, checking the monitors posted up near his bed.

"Dr. Keel, what is happening? He's on fire! And it looks like he's having a seizure!"

"He's reacting to the Loganyte. We need to move fast."

"Spencer? Can you hear me? Stay with me! Spencer..." said Juan Miguel, but his voice already seemed so far away. Blackwelder fell backward into his bed, through his bed, and down into a long, narrow, dark tunnel, Juan Miguel's voice getting farther and farther away and softer by the second.

He was floating now, somehow suspended in air. Around him, a drum beat, faint and far off, and a soft whisper sang a melodic tune. It reminded him of his grandmother, of the songs she used to sing about her people in faraway villages, before she immigrated. Below him were himself and Juan Miguel. They lay on the floor of his quarters, tangled in a blanket, a half-eaten dinner about ten feet away. They were physically spent, their bodies beaded with sweat and bathed in the scent of ecstasy, each of them wearing a giddy expression. They cuddled closely so their bare skin could touch at every opportunity. Blackwelder gently kissed Juan Miguel on the forehead before drifting off to the most blissful sleep he'd ever experienced.

He remembered that night well. It had been their second date. After ending the first with an innocent handshake and an awkward hug, Blackwelder had been anxious to get Juan Miguel alone and away from prying eyes. But, having achieved that goal, Blackwelder found himself too nervous to make a move. Juan Miguel had made a joke about a chorizo sausage early in the night, though, which started to heat things up to the extent that they didn't even make it to the bed before they were all over each other.

Then the scene changed. Now he was floating over a giant expanse of white, his own ruined body lying prone in the snow. The stench of burning flesh wafted into his nostrils and made him gag. The drumming drew closer, grew more intense, and he could recognize the ghostly song now, could understand its meaning: it was a funeral dirge from Indioafrica, one of the thirteen Allied Earth Regions. Blackwelder was looking down on himself, about to die, cut off and alone. In a training exercise, not even in actual combat. He had anticipated that Fort Felix would be the death of him in about six months, had known it when he requested to leave the Barack. But not like this. This wasn't how he wanted to go.

"Spencer…"

Blackwelder opened his eyes. He was back in the hospital bed, with Juan Miguel at his side. Juan Miguel looked tired, drained, but he smiled at Blackwelder as if nothing in the galaxy could make him happier than to be right where he was.

"Hey," Blackwelder said groggily.

"Hey. I'm so glad you're finally awake." He tried to hide the trace of fear in his voice, but Blackwelder picked up on it.

"I feel like I'm fighting through a serious haze right now. What did they give me?" But he thought he knew the answer already.

"Loganyte. You were pretty badly burned from the electric shock—inside and out—but it's mostly healed now. You were unconscious for forty-eight hours, and then you had a bit of an episode… That was about three days ago."

"Damn," was all Blackwelder could manage.

"I knew you'd be fine," Juan Miguel said. Blackwelder spotted that lie too, but again decided to ignore it.

"And Chiu's leg?"

"He's all patched up. They've still got him in observation over in Lilac, though they'll probably release him today."

"I'm going to go see him," Blackwelder said, trying to get out of bed.

"Wait, are you sure?" Hovering awkwardly, Juan Miguel seemed unsure about whether or not to try to physically restrain Blackwelder.

"I'm fine." Blackwelder sat up, and his head spun. He blinked hard several times, trying to force his equilibrium to right itself through sheer will. "I'm just going to visit my men, then get back to my own quarters. I'll come see you soon. I promise."

Juan Miguel considered him for a moment, as if debating whether or not to stop him. He must have decided it was best not to get in the way, because he gave a solemn nod and left the room.

Though he struggled to pull himself out of the bed, and despite the fact that it took him several minutes to get comfortable standing fully upright, Blackwelder soon found himself feeling rather refreshed, his strength returning to him in earnest. He traded his robes for a pair of fatigues and a physical training T-shirt and made his way down the Lilac corridors. M-Dome was color-coded: Jade Hall was officer recovery rooms; Lilac Hall was for enlisted; and Azure Hall was for the civilians. The entrance to the hospital wing was a very light shade of gray, but the emergency and operating rooms were all bright yellow. Some nonsense about keeping the mood as positive as possible.

Blackwelder moved swiftly past the lightly purpled walls and the techs in matching robes. Seeing people visiting others who had fallen ill or had been injured made him think of Juan Miguel, and he felt guilty for it. He really had been overjoyed to wake up to Juan Miguel by his bedside. There was no one else he would have rathered. But in that moment, there were only two people he wanted to see. The first, to make sure he was okay. The second, to make sure he wasn't.

Blackwelder checked in with the nurse and found Chiu's room. He was still laid up in his bed, but he wasn't alone; all of Brant Squad was with him. De Silva leaned against the wall, the picture of cool, while Bonner and Bailey played hands of cards and Petrey poured several glasses of water.

"—but that's just the way they do things back in Central Asia, huh, Petrey?" De Silva said. Everyone laughed at the joke, even Petrey.

"Holy shit, Blackwelder! I mean, sir. Sorry, sir!" Bailey said, catching a glimpse of Blackwelder as he entered Chiu's hospital room. They all turned to face him, clearly glad to see him well.

"We'd heard you fried to a crisp, sir," Petrey said, handing Chiu a water.

"What are they putting in your IV?" Chiu asked. "And how do I get some?" They all laughed.

"Loganyte," Blackwelder said.

The gasp was audible. Even De Silva's expression was one of shock and disbelief.

"Loganyte? Sir, you must have been in really bad shape...for them to risk..." Bonner said. The mood dipped sharply.

"Fix your faces. I took a bit of a nap, but I'm the picture of health now, as you can see. So don't expect any soft treatment at our next training."

"That's what I like to hear," said a voice from behind them. Everyone turned to see the major standing in the doorway, backlit by the faint purple hues in the hallway. With his tall, slender frame and silver hair, the effect was eerie. Otherworldly, even. And not in a good way. He waved them all down as they sloppily tried to assemble a salute.

"Sir, what happened in there?" Blackwelder asked.

"Well, you'd know better than me," Page said, leading Blackwelder back into the hallway. "But it seems you were right: a catastrophic malfunction. Lieutenant Colonel Lee got your message and had the entire arena shut down inside of three minutes."

"But the safety protocols going offline...how could that have happened?"

Page's look was initially one of annoyance, but it smoothed quickly into apparent concern. "We're looking into it. Greene's probably still at the Deck." Page looked down at his watch. "I'll put him on it right now."

Major Page walked away, leaving Blackwelder still outside Chiu's room, but out of view of his crew. He realized that Brant Squad had been whispering while he talked to the major, but with some effort, he was able to make out what they were saying.

"—gives me the creeps. Doesn't he?" De Silva said.

Bonner pressed her finger to her lips. "You can't talk about the major like that!"

"I'm just saying. And how is he still only a major? He definitely should have been promoted by now. The guy's like a hundred."

Chiu sat up a little straighter in his bed. "What I wanna know is how Greene's still a second lieutenant. You'd think after screwing up with us like that, he'd be busted back down to a private."

Bailey snorted with laughter. "With the added bonus of bed-pan duty!" They all laughed again.

"I tend to agree with you," Blackwelder whispered to himself. The time had come to find the second person on his list.

Flashing his ID to one of the privates posted at the east entrance to the hospital wing, Blackwelder quickly requisitioned a cart to drive himself to E-Dome, where he knew he'd find Greene smugly slurping shots at the Deck. Normally, he would walk; he wasn't really accustomed to making use of officer privileges like regular access to motorized transportation, but he was in a hurry. Blackwelder was angry, and he wanted to hold on to the heat of that anger. The walk would sap him, give him time to reconsider what he was planning to do. Or else, he'd run into a thousand people as he tried to cross B-Dome's "central hub," all of whom would be curious about what had happened in the Arena. Or he'd start thinking about Juan Miguel; his nurse had told him, as he hastily dressed to leave, that Juan Miguel had been at his bedside from the moment he was brought to the hospital. With that in his head, he knew it would be impossible to hold a negative thought. No, just this once, he decided he'd act like an officer.

Once inside E-Dome, the cart barely come to a stop before he leapt from it. He couldn't be bothered to check it back in. He thought of Chiu bleeding in the snow, and his feet moved more swiftly, carrying him past the mess hall, past the Cave. He thought of himself, electrocuted, and severely so, considering they'd decided to use the miracle drug Loganyte, which eight times out of ten resulted in a full recovery, but 20 percent of the time killed you stone dead. His feet moved more quickly still, past the commissary, past the post office. He thought of Burton, De Silva, Bailey, all of them, poisoned and frozen to death, the pathetic little squad no one could be bothered to care about, left to die like, like...well, like Elumerians.

At last, his anger had brought him to the Deck. From the entrance, he scanned the crowd, chatty and boisterous as always, until he found his prey. Greene was sitting at a table with two other men that Blackwelder vaguely recognized from around. They seemed as pleased with themselves as ever, but Greene appeared distracted and unenthused; he stared down at the table, his beer still mostly full.

"Greene," Blackwelder shouted. Like a Wild West saloon, the bar fell silent. Every head turned in Blackwelder's direction.

Greene looked up, a jumbled mix of emotions crossing his face. The confusion faded quickly, though, and his visage became resolute. "Blackwelder," he said, getting to his feet. "I had a feeling you'd come looking for me. You wanna take this some pla—"

"You son of a bitch!" Blackwelder suddenly appeared in front of Greene as if no physical space had ever existed between them. He punctuated his declaration with a right cross that staggered the second lieutenant.

"My men and I almost died in there! Where the hell were you?"

"I think you want to check yourself, Warrant Officer. We're not in J-Dome," Greene said, deliberately getting to his feet. He checked his bottom lip for blood but found none.

"I don't give a shit about your bars and stars, Greene. The only thing I want to hear from you is an explanation."

Greene looked back at his cronies. They shot glances between each other that Blackwelder couldn't make out, not that he was particularly focused on what they might be thinking.

"The only explanation you'll get from me is the one I gave you before you went in," Greene said. "You and your men couldn't cut it. There's a reason they're the only squad without a permanent squad commander; they're pathetic. And you're about as overrated as they come."

Blackwelder clenched his fists. "Say one more word about Brant Squad and I will end you."

"You want to play it that way? Fine. It's too bad those Fish Faces didn't finish you and your third-rate particulate monkeys off when they had the chance. Though, from what I hear, they came pretty damn close. So much for making Fort Felix proud!" His two buddies laughed loudly. A couple other people let out a low chuckle here and there. "Guess the holograms were just too much for your men. You all deserve each other."

Sufficiently baited, Blackwelder stepped in with another powerful swing, but Greene was ready for him this time. He deflected the shot and returned a gut-face punch combo that sent Blackwelder backward over a table. Blackwelder got back on his feet and immediately returned to the fight. They traded several mutually blocked jabs until Blackwelder landed a left-right combo, followed by an uppercut that sent Greene to the floor. His buddies tried to jump in, but Sergeant Major Burton had appeared as if from nowhere, standing between them and the circle that had formed a perimeter around the fighters. One shake of her head, and they immediately stepped down.

Greene righted himself and rushed Blackwelder, bowling them both over, but moving them more toward the open space near the entrance of the bar. They wrestled now, sneaking in as many close-body blows as they could. Greene untwisted himself from Blackwelder's grasp and was the first to find his footing again. He attempted to yank Blackwelder from the floor, but was met by a swift kick in the gut, which sent him right back down. Now Blackwelder was on his feet, closing in.

"That's enough."

Blackwelder stopped dead in his tracks. He turned to see none other than General Kilmer, the commanding officer of all of Fort Felix. The general was only average height and build, but his presence was massive. Blackwelder felt glued to his spot; he couldn't have continued fighting if he'd wanted to. The general was clean-shaven and had traces of gray in his mostly brown hair, and he stood stiffly with his hands folded behind his back. Blackwelder had seen the general before, at select staff meetings or at general assemblies, but he'd never had occasion to have a conversation with the man. He had no reason to believe the general even knew his name, except for the fact that Blackwelder's Area Commander, Lieutenant Colonel Lee, was standing right beside him.

"I understand you and your men have had a very difficult experience. We'll get to the bottom of what happened, don't you worry. In the meantime, you need your rest," General Kilmer said. And it was clear to all that the matter was closed.

"I'll take him back to his quarters, General," Juan Miguel said. Busy with the fighting as he'd been, Blackwelder hadn't noticed Juan Miguel's arrival either.

Greene's lackeys helped him back to his feet. For a moment, he and Blackwelder locked eyes, but Blackwelder was unable to read them. Juan Miguel gave a soft tug on Blackwelder's shoulder. Blackwelder's chest heaved as blood rushed to his head, his pulse thundering in his ears. He nodded, and allowed Juan Miguel to lead him out of the Deck.

JUAN MIGUEL AND Blackwelder made the short trip from the Deck to I-Dome, where the civilian staff's living quarters were located. Fort Felix actually employed several non-military Allied Earth citizens, including IT specialists, technicians, medical staff, and the majority of the workers in the commons. They walked down the long hall off the main entrance, lined with doors leading to individual living spaces not much bigger than a college dorm room. At the end of the hall, they turned a corner that led to a small alcove with a single door. It was marked C01 and had the letters JMA displayed above the call box. Juan Miguel waved his hand in front of the sensor on the call box, and the door slid open.

"This may have escaped your notice," Blackwelder said as he entered, "but these aren't my quarters."

"No? Well, I suppose we must have taken a wrong turn somewhere." He walked over to a cabinet and started to riffle through it.

Juan Miguel's quarters were large by dormitory standards; not obnoxiously so, but it was a significant amount of space for one person. The door opened on an antechamber that led to the living room, straight ahead, or a dining area to the right that could comfortably seat four. To the left was a small nook that Juan Miguel had set up as a secondary office space. In the living room, there was a couch shaped like a U that touched the wall on three sides and opened on a large coffee table. A massive screen adorned the nearby wall. On the wall across from the screen hung a large flag with two stripes—one dark blue and one yellow—and a seal in the middle that consisted of two red-bladed swords with a golden crown between them, and the letter *S* floating just above the crown, all suspended in a white circle. Blackwelder had learned way back in basic training that it represented one of the thirteen regions of the Allied Earth government, but he couldn't remember exactly which one.

Juan Miguel reappeared with some medical supplies. "Have a seat. Let's get you cleaned up."

Blackwelder sat on the couch, and Juan Miguel sat down very close to him. After he poured some solution onto a rag, Juan Miguel dabbed Blackwelder's lip, which was bleeding from his fight.

"I still can't believe that you did that," Juan Miguel said.

"Greene deserves worse." He held perfectly still as Juan Miguel carefully cleaned his wound. "It was his job to watch out for us. If he'd been monitoring us, things never would have gotten so out of hand. I'm not exaggerating when I say we could have died in there. I almost did."

"I know," Juan Miguel said solemnly. "Here."

Juan Miguel handed Blackwelder a cold compress to hold against his cheek, where dark purple bands had formed. The cold stung his skin at first, but his face immediately began to feel better. As he held the compress, his attention fell on the flag again.

"Do you recognize it?" Juan Miguel asked.

"I know I should, but I confess my world geography skills are pretty pathetic."

"It's the flag of the Tegucigalpan Empire, my home region. What, before the war began, was known as Central America and Colombia. I haven't told you this, but the empire's the reason I'm here, really."

"How do you mean? I thought the Tridecagon was responsible for assigning ambassadors."

"They are... It's kind of a long story."

"I'm not going anywhere," Blackwelder said.

Juan Miguel smiled warmly. "My father, Jose Manuel Arías—I know," he said at Blackwelder's curious expression, "it's like we're twins—haha. Anyway, he has the distinct pleasure of serving the Tridecagon as the senator to the Tegucigalpan Empire. I can't tell you the number of times he said those exact words to me. It's a position he only holds because, growing up, he was best friends with Francisco Gregorio Salazar, currently known as Emperor Gregorio II. Before the Elumerians attacked, our previous emperor, Gregorio I, was just General Carlos Gregorio Salazar, a military dictator from El Salvador whose armies were spreading like a cancer throughout the Central American countries. A cancer the rest of the world powers had chosen to ignore. Well, of course the war started and everything changed: everyone stopped fighting each other and turned their attention to the skies. The general's conquest was over. The countries he'd been at war with surrendered, and he declared himself emperor. My father then parlayed his close friendship with the emperor's son into a position as the second most powerful man in Central America. He cemented that position by negotiating a senate-approved expansion of our territory, so that now the empire includes all of the Caribbean Islands, except for Cuba.

"But that wasn't enough for my father. He didn't just want power. He wanted a legacy. He wanted to be royalty, like his friend. So when the emperor died, my father talked the new emperor into an arranged marriage between Crown Princess Laura Francisca and me."

"But, you're..." Blackwelder began.

"Gay. Yes. And my father knew it. But he didn't care. He'd demanded that I keep my private life discreet due to his political career, but my sexuality had always been sort of an open secret. When he realized he could become the grandfather of a future monarch, though, my discretion wasn't enough anymore."

"What did you do?"

"I refused, of course. I had no intention of spending the rest of my life in a lie just to serve my father's inflated ego and unchecked ambition. Besides, no one stopped to think about Laura's end of the deal. We both grew up in service to our fathers, so she understood duty. And since we are actually friends, she said she'd be willing to go through with it. Better me than the son of some other random political ally. But, I don't know, I didn't want to do that to her, trap her in a loveless, sexless marriage."

"So you turned down the chance to marry the future empress. I'm sure your father loved that."

"Oh, he did. He was so pleased that he used his influence as chair of the War Appropriations Committee to make me an official senatorial ambassador to a military command. It's a fluff position that senators hand out to their friends so they can take a 'work-ation' to a destination base like Oahu or Dubai. But my father pulled some strings and got me sent out here, to the end of the universe. So he could be sure he wouldn't have to look at the worthless son who had selfishly destroyed his dreams."

"It's an honorary position, though, right? You didn't have to accept it."

"He made it clear that, if I didn't, he would completely cut me off and make life in the empire very difficult for me. Which I'm sure would have given him more pleasure, to be able to take a more active role in my daily suffering. I imagine he expects me to die out here, but that's not going to happen. I'm going to survive his little punishment, go back home, and rub it in his face."

"But you're his son; you don't really think he wants you dead, do you?"

"I don't know, Spencer," Juan Miguel said, letting out a heavy sigh. "I guess not. But he hated me enough to send me here. You don't send someone whose well-being you're especially concerned about to the space colonies."

"I suppose." He was reminded of the conversation he had had when he told his friends on the AES Barack that he was transferring to Triton. They had certainly shared Juan Miguel's opinion. "But I just can't imagine that anyone, even your power-hungry father, could wish real harm on someone like you. Someone so...wonderful."

The comment seemed to catch Juan Miguel off guard.

Blackwelder put his hand on Juan Miguel's leg. "The nurse told me what you did, how you stayed with me the whole time. I didn't get a chance to say thank you."

"You sent me an unfinished message," Juan Miguel said, moving in a little closer. "I wanted to be sure I was there to hear the rest."

"So you got that. I was wondering. I was scared in the Arena, of many things, but especially of the idea that I'd never see you again. But even with that, I didn't know it for sure until I woke up and saw you sitting next to me in the hospital."

"Didn't know what?" Juan Miguel asked, his breath catching.

"That I am falling in love with you." Blackwelder moved in slowly until their faces were millimeters apart, their anticipatory breaths warming each other's cheeks. He kissed Juan Miguel, gently at first, as he was still a little sensitive from the fight, and then more forcefully, as their tongues met and grappled with each other.

Blackwelder eased Juan Miguel onto his back on the couch and hovered over him for a moment, their eyes locked, before he began to kiss him again. He kissed Juan Miguel's lips, his cheeks, his neck; he tickled Juan Miguel's ears with his tongue and trailed it down the side of his neck to his collarbone, while he worked furiously to unbutton Juan Miguel's shirt. Blackwelder pushed back the flaps of fabric, exposing the ambassador's bare chest, and then picked up the trail again, pausing at the pecs to run rings around his nipples. Juan Miguel shivered.

"Oh, you like that, huh?" Blackwelder said, giving his left nipple a playful nibble. Juan Miguel let out a soft moan in the affirmative. Blackwelder continued on his path down Juan Miguel's chest. He rubbed his cheeks against the soft hair on Juan Miguel's stomach as he reached for his belt.

They disrobed each other, grabbing at fabric and pulling it this way and that until it yielded. Juan Miguel pushed Blackwelder into a standing position so he could more easily pull his pants down. Once he'd exposed Blackwelder, he slid from the couch to his knees and gripped Blackwelder's thighs tightly as they connected. Blackwelder trembled with pleasure and excitement as Juan Miguel explored his body with his lips, his tongue, his warm wet mouth. Blackwelder's vocabulary was reduced to the word *yes* in an increasingly urgent tone as he wrapped Juan Miguel's hair around his fingers.

Suddenly, Juan Miguel stood up. He pressed his bare chest to Blackwelder's back, wrapped his arms around Blackwelder, gripping him tightly, and planted kisses on the back of his neck. Each kiss seemed to make Blackwelder more and more relaxed. Steering him from behind, Juan Miguel manuevered Blackwelder into the bedroom. They disentangled themselves only long enough to get into the covers. Once there, Juan Miguel wrapped himself around Blackwelder again, and peppered Blackwelder with kisses. His temperature rose as Juan Miguel held him close and gently glided his fingertips over the surface of his skin. Juan Miguel brushed the small of his back, and Blackwelder's heart skipped a beat. It had been quite a while since anyone had touched him there, and even though it had startled him, Blackwelder wanted nothing more than for the sensation to continue. Juan Miguel withdrew his hand, though, moistened his pointer and middle fingers with his saliva, and raised Blackwelder's right leg just enough to gain access. Blackwelder moaned softly, his back arching involuntarily.

Juan Miguel whispered in his ear: "Do you want to keep going?"

"Yes," Blackwelder consented and wrapped his legs around Juan Miguel's waist, his thighs resting on the top of Juan Miguel's glutes.

Juan Miguel brought his fingers up to his lips to wet them again and positioned himself above Blackwelder.

"Be gentle," Blackwelder whispered.

"I will." Juan Miguel gripped Blackwelder's hips tightly and pressed their bodies together with a tender thrust.

Blackwelder gripped Juan Miguel's shoulders desperately as an intense wave of pleasure washed over him. His skin tingled as if electric sparks were racing along the surface of his body, crowning at the top of his head. With each thrust, Blackwelder's ecstasy magnified, their flesh folding into each other as they finally became one.

IN THE COMMISSARY, Blackwelder grabbed some snacks from one of the shelves. The mess hall had been closed for hours, but there was always some prepackaged food items available to those seeking a late-night snack. He and Juan Miguel had already made love twice and were taking a little break in order to refuel. He didn't think anything could wrest the smile from his face, until he saw that he wasn't alone. Sec. Lt. Greene had just walked in.

They stared at each other for a moment. Blackwelder felt anger rising inside him, despite his recent release; perhaps he wasn't done with their fight after all. Greene, however, didn't seem to reciprocate that feeling. He broke their stare, looking away first.

"Definitely wasn't expecting to run into you," Greene said.

Blackwelder turned back to the shelf and continued to throw items into his basket, a bit more forcefully than he'd done previously.

"Since we're here, though," Greene continued, "I just wanted to say, I really am sorry about what happened in the Arena. It would have been...awful, if anything had happened to you all."

"What it would have been is your fault," Blackwelder snapped. "You were on monitor duty. You were supposed to be looking out for us. I knew you had a problem with me, but I had no idea you'd take it this far."

"It's not like that," Greene said. "I wasn't thrilled to get that assignment, especially after what happened with our squads, but I wouldn't intentionally let anything happen to you or your squad."

"Thrilled or not, it was your fucking job! On your honor as a soldier, as an officer, I should be able to count on you to do your job, regardless of anything else!"

"I did my job," Greene said without a trace of aggression. "After the simulation started, I was ordered to scale back my hours for monitor duty. I didn't want to be there anyway, so I gladly complied. I didn't think twice about it."

"You were ordered...by whom? And why would they tell you to do that?"

Greene just looked at Blackwelder. He didn't answer the question, not that he needed to. There were only a couple of people who could give him a training activity-related order, and only one who would. And, given the result, the why seemed fairly obvious as well. Without another word, Greene turned and left Blackwelder alone in the commissary.

Chapter Eight: Other Duties as Assigned

"GOOD MORNING, BEAUTIFUL," Blackwelder said as Juan Miguel stirred, slowly returning to consciousness. Blackwelder gently stroked his cheek.

"You're up early," Juan Miguel said.

In truth, Blackwelder had been awake for hours. He'd steadied himself by watching Juan Miguel as he slept, attempting, to no discernible level of success, to count the hairs on Juan Miguel's head. Inside, the vicious speed of his thoughts would not let him rest.

"You're still thinking about what Greene said, aren't you?"

"I can't help it. He basically told me there was a traitor right here on the base."

"That is not what he said."

"You're right. It's what he didn't say."

"And you trust Greene? He's about to be under investigation for dereliction of duty. He'd say anything, I'm sure. Besides, everything that happened in there can be explained by an equipment or system failure. You're not the first person on this base to almost freeze to death in those suits, for instance."

"That's all true. Except for the safety protocols. I can't imagine the amount of system damage that would have to occur for those to go offline on their own. If that had happened, everyone on this base would be in imminent danger. That's the sort of thing that happens right after the entire computer system gains sentience and right before it vents us all into space."

"But that's not what you're really worried about it."

"No?"

"No. What you're really worried about is the same thing that I am; that, if Greene's telling the truth, it means a superior gave him the order. Someone whose orders he wouldn't think to question."

"The XO—Major Page." Blackwelder paused for a moment. The declaration washed over him. "I can't believe I said that aloud."

"Don't worry; it's not like my quarters are bugged. At least, I don't think they are. That's going to be really awkward for someone after last night."

Blackwelder smiled.

"Let's just talk about something else."

"What do you know about the Junk Star?" Blackwelder asked.

"I'm not sure that's better."

"But it is something else."

"Probably a great deal more than I should." Juan Miguel sat up in the bed. "What do you know about it?"

"I don't remember much. Just that it was the supposed to be the 'savior of mankind' or some such. Basically a new place to put all our trash."

"It was exactly that, a man-made satellite whose sole purpose was to be a landfill. Layer upon layer of waste compressed and held in place with magnetic fields. It got to be the size of a small island before we finally had to cut it loose from our orbit. The United Nations set it adrift into space, never to be seen or heard from again."

"Exactly. Astro-Command said the Junk Star got incinerated in the sun's orbit. So what could it possibly have to do with the Elumerians?"

Juan Miguel paused. Blackwelder could see the wheels turning in his mind, whether or not he would "spin" his answer, or be honest. He wondered if he was about to finally meet Juan Miguel the politician.

"It turns out Astro-Command wasn't completely honest. The Junk Star was headed for the sun, but a guidance malfunction led it off course. It basically did a slingshot around the sun toward the outer Solara-Neuf. Then, it vanished just beyond Neptune space."

"Here? Where the aliens disappeared after the first waves of the war? That's a strange coincidence," Blackwelder said, his voice already heavy with disbelief.

"What very few in the military and practically no one outside of the highest ranking members of government know is that the Elumerians entered our solar system through a wormhole, and escaped it the same way. More importantly, Chief Astronomer Leilani knew of the wormhole's existence before the Elumerians attacked. They discovered it while searching for the missing Junk Star. Astro-Command sent a probe in after the Junk Star, mostly out of curiosity. They thought that they might be able to manipulate the wormhole in some way. But when the probe emerged on the other side, it recorded a planet that had been devastated by what appeared to be the impact of an island-sized asteroid."

"No…"

"The Junk Star appeared in Elumerian space, flew into the planet's orbit, and crashed down on the unsuspecting beings below. The impact alone had unimaginable consequences, but remember what the Junk Star actually is."

"Literally a huge pile of garbage?"

"A planet's worth of trash and pollution, detonated on your world like ten nuclear bombs."

Blackwelder steepled his fingers under his chin. "We started this war. Even if accidentally, we fired the first shot," he said.

"Indeed. Now imagine if the citizens of Allied Earth knew it, that our government itself was responsible for this war. But which government? The United States for coming up with the idea? The Chinese for funding it? The Indians for building and launching it? Or the United Nations for sanctioning the whole project? Finger pointing and blame would dominate the international conversation, and just like that, the Allied Earth is finished. Without Allied Earth, we've got no global defense plan. The Elumerians show up, and it's pretty much the end of the world."

"And with all of Allied Earth's focus on the Elumerians, there's hardly anyone paying attention to planetary issues, like the Retribution. I…I had no idea …."

"There's a lot that goes on above the 'Point and Shoot' level. My father made me into a politician; he'll live to regret that."

"Wow. The 'Point and Shoot level'? That's a little condescending, don't you think? Not to mention the fact that it trivializes the fact that we put our very lives on the line each day."

Blackwelder freed himself from the covers and moved toward the edge of the bed. "As soldiers, I know we're expected to follow orders without question, but that doesn't stop us from thinking outside the box. From thinking about what's going on behind the scenes. The Elumerians, the Retribution… nothing's quite what it seems."

"Wait." Juan Miguel grabbed Blackwelder's arm. "I didn't mean it like that. I was borrowing a phrase… I shouldn't have, wasn't thinking. I'm sorry."

Blackwelder debated giving Juan Miguel a hard time, but the sad, apologetic look on his face made him melt. "Oh all right. I'll forgive you this time. I should get going though. I'm sure Lieutenant Colonel Lee will want to debrief me properly."

"Okay. Dinner later?" Juan Miguel asked sheepishly.

Blackwelder leaned in for a kiss as he walked out, the door sliding closed behind him.

"BARBARA, RIGBERTO," JUAN Miguel said as he walked past the commissary. He waved brightly.

"Good Morning, Juan Miguel," they both said back. He paused for just a moment before continuing on his way.

E-Dome, in many ways, resembled an airport terminal, with its long, grand hallway with the hard tile floor and bleached fluorescent lighting. The commissary, like a duty-free store, stood off to one side, directly across from a seldom-visited book and gift shop. All of E-Dome was relatively quiet at this time of morning, though; the mess hall wasn't scheduled to begin serving breakfast for another hour.

The commons, equidistant from the Cave and the Deck, was a very large space set up to resemble a living room. Several squashy brown armchairs dotted the room's landscape and were huddled in little pods around small coffee tables. Longer couches were placed along the walls around the room. 3-D video game stations were set up in the rear of the room for those so inclined, but in the front of the room were two permanent chess stations. The true classics, it seemed, were never far from the popular conscience.

"Good morning, Ambassador," said a custodial worker as Juan Miguel walked past. "You certainly look stellar this morning."

"Thank you, Tumi," he said with a smile. He smoothed the front of his jacket. He was dressed for business with a suit, tie, and well-polished shoes. He wore a pin, the Allied Earth logo, on his lapel. "You're looking well, too. And this place: spotless as ever. We are certainly going to miss you."

"Thank you, sir," she said, returning some supplies to her cart. "I'll be sad to go, but I must admit, I'm excited about Lunar 1!"

"It's a great opportunity. Lunar 1 is Allied Earth's premiere space colony. Definitely a step up from this place."

"Well, I'm getting older, too. It would be nice to look out the window and see Earth every now and then."

"Of course. The going-away party is still on for next Friday! Enjoy the rest of your day," he said, moving on. He paused a few steps beyond the commons, though. He considered something a moment, and then returned.

"Tumi, might I ask a favor?" He paused briefly before continuing. "I do so value your assistance." He gave a slight nod, signaling his intentional use of the code phrase he'd only had occasion to use once before.

"Of course, Ambassador," Tumi said, suddenly serious. "Anything I can do to help you, you know that." The room was empty, but she looked around anyway as if she half expected someone to appear. She moved closer to Juan Miguel.

"Thank you. Would you, and the other custodial staff, do an extra round at the offices of the Weapons Training Battalion? I've gotten some complaints from the XO there."

Tumi nodded solemnly. "Certainly, Ambassador."

"Thanks again."

Juan Miguel continued toward the end of the hall until he came to the post office. Communications had evolved dramatically over the centuries, and yet the name had remained as a nostalgic link to the past. Though almost everyone on the base had some sort of personal communication device, none of those devices were able to transmit or receive any signals outside of Neptune space. There were only two places in Fort Felix capable of establishing two-way communications from anywhere beyond the base: the A-Dome, where the base command offices were located, and the post office. So anyone trying to get a nonwork personal message, whether it be from one of the Allied Earth ships, one of the other bases, or Earth itself, had to visit the Postmaster.

"Good morning, Postmaster Zeng," Juan Miguel said. Zeng, the woman behind the counter, was an older but robust Chinese woman who wore thick black glasses with gold etchings on the side and a strict hair bun.

"Good morning, Ambassador Arías," she said, eying him over the rim of her glasses.

"How is exile treating you today?"

"About as well as it's treating you, I'd imagine. Though, on second thought, perhaps not as well...?"

"Spencer?" Juan Miguel asked, already blushing hard.

"Of course. How's it going?"

His blush deepened. "Wonderfully.

"Then I'm very happy for you. Warrant Officer Blackwelder seems like a very nice and capable young man from what I've heard. But you didn't come here to talk about your new boyfriend."

"Boyfriend...." He liked the sound of the word in his mouth. "No, not directly anyway." He looked over his shoulder toward the open hallway. There was still no one around. "I came to speak with you about some undelivered mail."

"Well. I take customer service very seriously, Ambassador. Better step into my office."

At the end of the counter was a door that led to a back office. Zeng gestured toward it, and Juan Miguel entered the room. Zeng followed him closely. Once they were both inside, she tapped the metal bracelet on her wrist. A soft humming noise enveloped the room. It was loud enough to be noticeable, but not so loud as to be distracting.

"Okay, distortion field is active. You can speak freely."

Juan Miguel took a moment to compose himself. Though he was prepared, he didn't think he'd ever need to utter the words he was about to say. "Spencer believes that we've got a traitor on base."

"And you think it may be a member of the Retribution?"

"Most likely. Spencer said the Elumerian projections in the Arena yelled out 'Junk Star' right before the safety protocols mysteriously went offline. Seems like quite the coincidence."

Zeng shook her head and waved her pointer finger at Juan Miguel. "If the spy game has taught me anything, it's that true coincidences are very few and far between. It's been difficult collecting information since they shipped me way out here. Anything from your contacts?"

"I sent a coded message to Princess Laura from my office yesterday. And I got an automated ping saying I had a private reply ready."

"Well, let's check." She tapped her bracelet again as they exited her private office, returning to the counter in the post office. Once back at the desk, Zeng began typing into the computer console. "Here it is. Just type in your download code."

A virtual keypad appeared on the counter in front of Juan Miguel. He punched in a short sequence of numbers. When he was finished, the pad disappeared and a blue light activated on the screen behind Zeng. Less than a minute later, a small flat disc about an inch wide was ejected.

"Here you are." Zeng handed him the disc. "Booth seven, please."

"Thanks."

Juan Miguel took the disc and headed for the cylindrical pods that occupied the majority of the post office. The pods, which resembled single-serving photo booths, allowed users to use the full holographic interface to experience their interplanetary mail. The booths were all networked to the main computer, so Zeng could activate the playback from her station. All of them except Booth 7. Booth 7 was "broken" and could only be operated manually.

Juan Miguel took a seat inside the booth and pulled the hatch shut. He inserted the disc, and the booth immediately came to life. The inside of the booth temporarily went pitch black before coming online, and a moment later, Juan Miguel's virtual environment placed him at a desk in a large office, sitting across from a young woman in a high-collared dress shirt with her hair straight and down to her shoulders. She had an unmistakably regal air about her.

"My dearest Juan Miguel. I'll be brief," she said, speaking in Spanish. The image of the princess looked directly at him, as if he were actually sitting at her desk in the palace back on Earth. He could hear the swishing of the curtains as air blew in from an open window. He could even smell Laura's perfume, a sensory tell they'd decided on to ensure the authenticity of her messages. The Tegucigalpan flag, the same one that hung on his bedroom wall, was displayed behind her.

"I ran your question past my team in Imperial Intelligence. They confirmed that there are likely three Retribution agents and/or small cells implanted at different space bases. The probable locations are Mars, Triton, and either the Barack, or one of her sister warships. So yes, it's plausible that you may have a traitor on your base. There's no intelligence on what they may be planning, so as ever, be careful. I hope to see you again soon." And with that, the simulation faded away, returning Juan Miguel to the plain gray chamber.

"Laura confirms that Fort Felix...might have an infestation," Juan Miguel said, again carefully looking around the room. He walked back to Zeng's station.

"Perhaps Major Page's office should be checked for those unwanted guests?"

"Why would you say that?" Juan Miguel asked, looking around himself reflexively.

"Given the incident in the Arena, it stands to reason that some little critters may have gotten into the system and caused those malfunctions. Since the major gives most of the direct orders in that area, you want to make sure he stays comfortable. That his workspace is not...compromised."

"Yes, that does seem logical. Well reasoned, Postmaster Zeng."

"A spy in exile is still a spy, Ambassador," she whispered softly with a wink.

"I've asked the custodial crew to take a closer look on the major's behalf. We certainly wouldn't want any bugs slipping through our fingers."

"Indeed."

"You know, I bet it's a lovely day on Mars," Juan Miguel said. "Could you send the Mars base commander, General Shah, my regards? Let her know that I'm thinking of her, please."

"Of course.".

"Thank you. Well, I've got to be getting to an appointment in A-Dome."

"Good luck with your next call," Zeng said, not looking up from her console. Juan Miguel smiled as he made his way back to the hallway.

"THE GENERAL WILL see you now," the assistant said to Juan Miguel. He'd been waiting for about five minutes for his scheduled meeting with Fort Felix's commanding officer. The assistant ushered him into the general's office, which was decidedly plain and unadorned. There was a desk, a table with three chairs pulled up to it, and an Allied Earth flag mounted on the wall. A wall-sized view screen hung across from the general's desk. A golden *T* rotated in the center of the idle screen, the mark of the Tridecagon.

"He's on the line," the general said, extending his hand to shake Juan Miguel's.

"Thank you, General. I deeply appreciate your help in this."

"I'll do whatever is necessary to ensure the well-being of my base and my men," the general said. He took his seat. After a solemn nod to Juan Miguel, he tapped a button on his desk, revealing the "he" he'd spoken of earlier.

"Greetings, General Kilmer."

"And to you too, Senator Arías," Juan Miguel said as he casually walked into view. Juan Miguel's father, Senator Jose Manuel Arías, stared back at his son with an expression of disbelief. Juan Miguel and his father had similarly shaped noses but, aside from that, looked nothing alike. The senator's hair was combed into a helmetlike style, and the crinkles around his eyes and deep lines in his forehead adorned an otherwise youthful-looking face. Juan Miguel could at least look forward to aging gracefully.

"Ambassador. I wasn't expecting you to be on this call," said the senator.

"You haven't been returning my communications, Senator, so the general was kind enough to intercede."

"Oh Juan Miguel, I would hope you'd know better than to pester the general with your whining—"

"This is a legitimate military matter, Senator. Despite the example set for me, I do not condone allowing personal discord to interfere with my professional responsibilities."

The senator was about to reply but seemed to lose his words. He glanced over at the general, who for his part was betraying no emotion.

"Now then"there's been an incident here at Fort Felix."

"What sort of incident?"

"A training accident. An entire squad of soldiers was nearly killed due to multiple system and equipment failures, all of which could have been prevented."

The senator clicked his tongue impatiently. "General Kilmer has a capable, dedicated staff.I am confident that he's more than able to manage any situation that may arise."

"With all due respect to the general and his impeccable team, there's only so much they can do with outdated technology and substandard equipment! The suits can't hold a sufficient charge to keep their wearers from freezing to death. The oxygen filters needed to be replaced six months ago. Not patched, not recycled, replaced. The operating systems in three different domes need critical upgrades, including the security system in the hangar bay. And due to the decreasing variety of options for successful treatment, the medical team here has started using Loganyte in more cases—with predictable outcomes. As leader of the War Appropriations Committee, it is your responsibility to ensure that *all* of Allied Earth's space colonies and bases are well provided for, not just your show pony flagship base Lunar 1."

"How dare you presume to lecture me on my responsibilities. Remember your place, Ambassador."

"I am well aware of my place, Senator. I am Fort Felix's official liaison to the Tridecagon, a fact you are well aware of, as I am here under your appointment. It is my duty to communicate the needs of this base and its people to our government, and in this time of war, the needs of this base are synonymous with the needs of all of Allied Earth. Now, 'my place,' as you pointed out, actually entitles me to bring my concerns directly to the entire Tridecagon. I contacted you first as a courtesy, Senator, but if you would prefer, if you insist on continuing to operate as an obstruction on Allied Earth's path to victory, then I would be more than happy to exercise that right."

Struck silent again, the senator glared at his son. Juan Miguel was not intimidated and held the stare unflinchingly. After a few moments, the senator blinked first. Juan Miguel swallowed a smile.

"Fort Felix is the first base in this system, Senator, depending on your perspective. Our ability to function determines the security of our entire species," General Kilmer said.

"General Kilmer?"

"Yes, Senator?"

"Send me what you need. I will do everything in my power to ensure Fort Felix's needs are met at this critical time."

"Thank you, Senator. My XO will forward the requisition within the hour."

"Ambassador," the senator said coolly.

"Senator," Juan Miguel said with a slight nod. The senator cut the communication, and the screen went blank.

Juan Miguel let out a deep sigh. In his exhale, he seemed to lose a couple inches, his body returning to its normal state now that the danger has passed.

"You've just cut through in minutes what has taken me months using the proper channels." The general stood and walked from behind his desk.

"Well, that was why my position was created, to provide exactly this kind of support. It's too bad so few other ambassadors take their roles seriously."

"Despite whatever circumstance brought you here, Fort Felix is lucky to have you, Ambassador. You're an asset to this base," said General Kilmer. He shook Juan Miguel's hand again and gestured toward the door, his sign that this conference was concluded.

"Thank you, sir. There's one more thing, though. I know you would prefer hard facts to speculation, but this is too important not to inform you."

"What is it?"

"I believe there is a traitor on base, an agent working for the Retribution who means to sabotage our efforts. I believe this person is actually responsible for what happened in the Arena."

"Do you have a name?"

"No. I believe they are highly placed, but I don't have sufficient supporting evidence just yet."

"Bring me the name as soon as you can back it up. You'll go through the normal channels?" The general returned to his desk.

"Yes, sir."

"Then I look forward to hearing your report, Ambassador," the general said. He sat back down behind his desk, ending the conversation.

Chapter Nine: Reactions

BLACKWELDER PULLED JUAN Miguel's arms up over his head and used his own body weight to pin him against the wall. He kissed Juan Miguel deeply, hungrily, and then let his lips slip down to the crook of Juan Miguel's neck.

"That tickles," Juan Miguel whispered.

"I know," Blackwelder said, as he traced the outline of Juan Miguel's collarbone with his tongue. It had been a few weeks since their last encounter in Juan Miguel's quarters, and despite the fact that they literally lived at work—or perhaps because of it—Blackwelder had wasted no time, stealing every moment he could. Physically, he'd learned a great deal about Juan Miguel: how to touch him, where, just how much pressure he could apply before pleasure turned to pain. And from there, how long until the pain ceased to be arousing.

"We have to go. They'll be here any minute."

Blackwelder pouted. "I don't want to. Can't we just stay here?"

"This visit's kind of a big deal, so my absence will probably be noticed. Besides, don't you want to see your friend?"

"I do," Blackwelder pulled away. He leaned against the opposing wall, but as they were in a mechanical access port—a glorified gear closet— the additional space created was negligible. His back pressed against a cold metal valve and he readjusted, which brought him eye level to the small window in the port door. Blackwelder ducked as he saw a soldier walk by.

"You haven't spoken to her since you left the Barack?"

"No, I thought it best if I just cut all ties to him once I left the ship."

Juan Miguel raised an eyebrow. "Him?"

"Her, I mean. Lyta," he said quickly.

"You meant Robby."

Blackwelder's awareness of their confined space grew rapidly. He had, of course, mentioned his life on his former assignment, referenced the time he'd spent with Abernathy and Macke. But he had avoided getting too far into the depth of his and Macke's relationship.

"Well, I'm sure she'll be glad to see you."

"Yeah... So, anything new on Page?" Blackwelder adjusted his uniform. His shirt had come untucked from beneath his dark green uniform coat.

"Nothing concrete. He's disappeared off the radar for short periods of time, but other than that, my network hasn't been able to confirm any suspicious activity. You're sure Greene's *not* the guy?"

"Honestly? No. Except that Page's 'investigation' just cleared Greene of any culpability in the Arena incident. So unless the second lieutenant is somehow blackmailing the major, I would have to put my money back on Page. Here," he said, reaching for Juan Miguel's tie. He tightened it, tugged on his shirt collar, and smoothed his suit jacket. His hand rested over Juan Miguel's heart, where he'd pinned a golden squared *T* to his lapel.

"Don't want you walking out of here looking like someone shoved you in a locker," Blackwelder said.

Juan Miguel covered Blackwelder's hand with his own. "We should go, Spencer. Half the base will be in the hangar bay by now, if only to see what's going on."

"Sure you want to walk in together, then? People might talk."

"Please. All of Fort Felix already knows you're my boyfriend."

"You think everyone knows? That I'm your..." Conflicted, Blackwelder tried to smile and scowl at the same time, a deep blush creeping across his light copper-colored face.

"Captain Albermarle actually came up to congratulate me yesterday while I was having lunch at the Deck."

"He did? That's random. Albermarle's decent, though."

"He thinks highly of you, Spencer. And he's not the only one."

Blackwelder waved him off. "He's just happy his squad's shooting a little straighter, that's all. I've had his air group doing steady rotations in the simulator for like a week and half."

Juan Miguel sighed. "Don't do that."

"Do what?"

"Deflect the compliment."

Blackwelder started to say something but stopped.

"Tell me I'm wrong,"

"Let's just get going," Blackwelder peeked through the window and, seeing that the way was clear, slid open the port door.

A few minutes later, Blackwelder and Juan Miguel entered the hangar bay dome. The cavernous space was a sterile light gray, awash in LED lighting that could have been warmer, more pleasant, but was kept neutral to promote workplace efficiency. Or, at least that was what Blackwelder had been told by an engineering grunt one drunken night in the Cave. The floor was scuffed and scarred from the heavy crates of ammunition, military tech, and various supplies that had been dragged back and forth. The girders supporting the bay were shaped like hexagons. In each of the alcoves the hexagons created were various aircraft; smaller short-range ships were docked toward the rear of the bay, where Blackwelder had entered. These ships were generally used for medical transport or external maintenance work. The Cam fighters—Japanese-made space fighters with long, flat noses and smooth, sensible edges—were parked toward the front of the bay, as the expansive chamber stretched on to the massive sealed doors that separated the rest of the hangar from the air-locked landing runway, which was constantly displayed on monitors scattered throughout.

Several men and women were assembled in ranks. Members of the command staff, including General Kilmer and his XO, Colonel Tsui, were lined up in front of the assemblage, while representatives from the other key areas, Weapons Training, Headquarters & Support, and Military Police, were lined up behind them. Juan Miguel quickly brushed his hand across Blackwelder's shoulder as he moved away to join the command staff, taking up the spot on General Kilmer's left. Blackwelder glanced after him for just a moment before taking up his own place between Burton and Greene.

"Cutting it close there, Blackwelder," Greene said. "Though, I'm sure if you were running late, your boyfriend could just write you a note."

"Calm down, Greene; it's not like anyone almost died from completely avoidable complications during a training exercise."

Greene's resulting bug-eyed expression and Burton's smirk gave Blackwelder a great deal of satisfaction.

"So, good news or bad?" Blackwelder said to Burton, but when she didn't respond right away, he looked over to see that her gaze was fixed on a tall, thin redhead about twenty yards away who was hard at work unloading equipment from a transport. He stacked three heavy black crates on top of each other and glanced in the assemblage's direction. He flashed a smile.

"I wouldn't presume to know," Burton said. "You're more familiar with Admiral Vaughn than I am. But whatever it is, it must be very important for him to travel all this way."

"Yes, I suppose you're right," he said. He looked back over at the redhead, who was now stealing periodic glances at Burton. "That's Sergeant Wyatt over there, right? I think I ran into him once at the Cave. He seems in high spirits today, wouldn't you say?"

"I wouldn't presume to know," Burton said, standing a little taller. Blackwelder felt the temporary urge to high-five Burton, but knowing she would murder him for such an action, he let the idea slip away.

"The envoy from the AES Barack is making its final approach!" said a voice over the PA.

"Ten-hut!" snapped Colonel Tsui. They obeyed her commands instantly and all locked into place, prepared to greet their guests.

A loud but distant grinding sound reverberated through the metal structure as the outer doors of the hangar pulled open. As he was in attention, he could not turn to face the monitor, but from the corner of his eye, three ships flew into the outer hangar and touched down on the runway. In the middle was a slightly boxy transport ship bookended by two sleek Cam fighters. All three vessels bore the name AES Barack across their right wings. Once all three ships had come to a complete stop, the outer doors closed, and the antechamber repressurized. Now the inner hangar doors ground open, and they proceeded into the main area, the Cam fighter in the front of the procession pulling to one side so the transport could take the lead. It stopped a safe distance away from where General Kilmer waited, his hands patiently clasped behind his back.

A small security detail disembarked first. They were quickly followed by Admiral Vaughn, fleet commander for the four war-class Allied Earth ships currently stationed in the Solara-Saturn sector of the solar system, which included the Barack, the admiral's flagship, and the three other ships buoyed between Saturn and Neptune. Blackwelder had never dealt with the man personally, but he obviously knew who he was. He was much better acquainted, however, with the person who followed the admiral: Blackwelder's old friend, Lyta Abernathy. The light danced off the insignia pinned to her shoulders—a single gold bar with two silver stars instead of one, as he remembered. It looked like she had finally been promoted.

"Admiral Vaughn, it is my pleasure to welcome you to Fort Felix," General Kilmer said, extending his hand in greeting. Vaughn was a tall man with Afro-Mediterranean features and an apparently firm handshake, given the way the general's shoulder seemed to bounce while they shook.

"We appreciate your rolling out the welcome mat, General," Vaughn said. "This is Captain Abernathy, one our newest in Force Intelligence."

"General," Abernathy said as she saluted.

"Captain," Kilmer said, returning the gesture. "This is my number two, Colonel Tsui. And this is Ambassador Juan Miguel Arías—"

Suddenly, a voice—menacing, and filled with wrath—called out from the assemblage: "Death to the Allied Earth!"

The general and the admiral both turned to see who had spoken. Major Page stepped out of the line and took a couple steps toward the admiral before stopping.

"Page, what are you doing?" Lt. Col. Lee demanded.

"The days of false unification are numbered, Admiral. The Retribution shall not stop until the Tridecagon crumbles!"

"The Retribution—?" Kilmer began, but before he could finish his thought, a detonator slipped from Page's sleeve into his palm.

"Bomb!" one of the MPs yelled. Fort Felix's police and the Barack's security detail both pulled their weapons and aimed them at Major Page, but they were too late; Page had already pushed the button.

DARK SMOKE SWIRLED through two-thirds of the room, battling the breathable air into submission. A sickly orange light flitted about in his peripheral vision, flames dancing where people had previously been standing. Mouths moved, faces contorted in pain and twisted into shock and fear, but he couldn't make out what they were saying; the sounds reaching Blackwelder were far off and muffled to the point of indistinctness. Something terrible had happened.

Burton and Greene were crouched beside him; he still gripped their shoulders tightly, his fists filled with as much of their uniforms as he could grab. Not knowing from which direction the blast would come, Blackwelder had instinctively dropped down, making himself as small as possible. What startled him, though, was that he'd thought enough of

Greene to take him with him. But Greene hadn't been the person Blackwelder wanted to save. His eyes stung from the smoke as he strained to see ahead. There, about twenty feet away, he spotted Juan Miguel. He was flat on his back, but he was moving, and in that instant, that was enough to keep Blackwelder sane. The general was lying close by, also apparently alive.

Another ten feet away, the admiral struggled to right himself. A body was splayed across him, a casualty of the blast. Blackwelder could tell from the uniform that the soldier had been a member of the admiral's security detail and not Abernathy, thankfully, who seemed to be coming to at the admiral's side. And then, striding through the smoke as if in slow motion, like a wraith, Blackwelder saw Page. His face was backlit by a ferocity Blackwelder could never have imagined seeing on the XO. He had done this. He was responsible for what was happening. He had tried to blow up the admiral and had failed miserably, instead only managing to create chaos and confusion, kill innocent bystanders, and completely displace the admiral's security.

Blackwelder understood. As he saw Page's arm rise into position with his sidearm primed and ready, he understood that Page had not made a mistake at all. His plan was unfolding exactly as he'd intended, and now there'd be no one steady enough to stand in his way.

Page let out a roar as a blue light hit him in the sternum and knocked him off his feet.

As life returned to the scene, all eyes turned to see Blackwelder, his L9 still trained on a defenseless Page. The Felix MPs that were still capable of it rushed over to Page, surrounding him.

"You stunned him?" Greene asked, getting back to his feet. "What a waste of laser fire. You should have killed the son of a bitch!"

"Not my call," Blackwelder said, meeting Kilmer's eye. The smoke scratched his throat as he spoke. "Besides, dead, he can't tell us anything."

"You will get nothing from me," Page said coolly. The fury that had blazed in his eyes moments ago seemed to have been thoroughly extinguished. The MPs pulled him back to his feet and cuffed his hands behind his back.

"My God," Lt. Col. Lee said, looking around the hangar. Bodies were littered around two distinct blast locations. Some of the soldiers were stirring, painfully, but most of them were not. Equipment had been blasted apart and reduced to shrapnel. Bloodstains had mixed with the smoke and ash and already started to blacken. A relatively small area of the hangar had been affected by the explosion, but it was a heavily populated one.

As the soldiers got their wits back, they attacked the small fires that still burned and tried to care for the people too injured to move as the medics finally rushed into view.

"Get him out of my sight," Lee said, her eyes flashing dangerously. After getting a nod from the general, the soldiers dragged Page from the hangar.

"Wyatt," Burton said. She ran after a medic in the direction of the first explosion, the three crates that Wyatt had been unloading. Blackwelder made to follow her, but Juan Miguel stopped him.

"Spencer, you're alright?" Juan Miguel said, panicked.

"Yeah, I'm okay. You?"

"Yes…" Juan Miguel looked as if he wanted to say something, but he was holding back. He quickly glanced at the general and the admiral. Blackwelder could see the wheels turning in his mind.

"Fuck it." Juan Miguel swooped in and kissed Blackwelder on the lips before wrapping him in a strong embrace. Over Juan Miguel's shoulder, Blackwelder could see the slightly startled look on Admiral Vaughn's face. But he wasn't on Vaughn's warship or even in his fleet anymore. Vaughn's personal opinion was no longer a subject about which Blackwelder needed to be concerned.

He hugged Juan Miguel back now, fully engaging in the embrace. "I'm okay."

General Kilmer cleared his throat.

"General, I'm glad to see you are also unharmed," Juan Miguel said as he disengaged from Blackwelder.

"Ambassador, could you and Colonel Tsui see the admiral and Captain Abernathy to A-Dome? I will join you after I've seen to the men."

"Of course," Juan Miguel said. He exited with the admiral and Abernathy in tow. As she passed, she gave Blackwelder a knowing look.

"You two, help the medics get the wounded back to M-Dome," General Kilmer said.

"Yes, sir!" Blackwelder and Greene yelled together. But as the general moved away toward one of the victims being triaged, Blackwelder's memory returned to him.

He ran off toward where Burton had gone. When he found her, she was standing a few feet away from a medic who seemed to be finishing up. Her patient, Sergeant Wyatt, wasn't moving. His red hair was slicked with blood to one side of his face, but otherwise, the young man looked as though he were sleeping.

"He's gone. I'm sorry," the medic said as she stood.

"Burton," Blackwelder said, turning to his friend. She stared down at Wyatt's lifeless body, her face the perfect picture of calm.

"On my honor, Arthur Page will never leave this base alive." Without another word, Sergeant Major Burton got up and took her leave.

Chapter Ten: Accountability

BLACKWELDER SLOUCHED IN his chair. His eyes glazed over as he stared halfheartedly at the holographic image before him: he was Commander Jack Indigo, tramping through the wild jungles of the Tegucigalpan rain forest on a mission to ruthlessly hunt down and destroy some treacherous insurgents. Human insurgents, almost as dangerous as the Elumerians themselves. The commons was not normally a place Blackwelder dwelled; all told, he'd probably spent as much time there as he'd spent in the Deck, and time spent playing the 3-D video games offered there was zero, as he would have, on any other occasion, much preferred a training simulation at J-Dome. On that night, though, the commons had been a means to an end, as the man who was once the best-dressed enlisted man in the Allied Earth Forces now hid in plain sight, a sad figure of an officer in a baggy T-shirt, sweatpants, and cap pulled low on his brow.

"I thought I might find you here," Abernathy said. Her hair fell loose now instead of the tight bun she'd worn the previous day when she arrived. She sat in the armchair next to Blackwelder. Upon seeing her, he sheepishly pulled off the headphones and removed the sensor gloves, and the projected image of Commander Jack Indigo vanished.

"Actually, this was the last place I would normally think to look, but fortunately, I ran into a Lieutenant Greene who had seen you hanging around here, apparently incognito," she said, gesturing to his clothing. "If I didn't know any better, I'd say you were avoiding me. But you wouldn't do that, right?"

"No, of course not! I'm here all the time. I was just—" He looked around the room; it was getting late, and the commons was nearly empty. "—just avoiding you," he confessed. "I'm sorry. I heard that you were in M-Dome getting checked out and I was going to meet you there, and then, I just..." He shook his head.

"You probably thought you'd be dead by now and that you'd never have to face me." Her voice was soft, but the edge to her tone was clear.

"Yes, actually. When I left the Barack, I did think...maybe even hoped—"

"You would have rather died here alone than tell me the truth? That doesn't say much about our friendship."

"I'm a terrible friend! Being with him, seeing you, pretending that I hadn't been with him; I couldn't take it. When I finally stopped for a minute to consider, I just got so disgusted with myself. I'd done this unforgivable thing, and I felt like I deserved to be punished. If I just could have been straight like everyone else—"

"Being gay was never the issue, Spencer, at least not between us. You lied to me, on virtually a daily basis. How could you betray me like that?"

"I don't have the words, Lyta," he said, barely able to meet her eye. "There's literally nothing I could say, except that I'm so, so sorry. It was heartless and cruel."

"It was," she said, her voice rising slightly. She quickly glanced around the room, and remembering they weren't entirely alone, she mastered herself. "And then you ran away like a selfish coward."

Blackwelder grimaced. Her words stung him, but he had no defense.

"I've struggled ever since I enlisted to figure out who I was and what I really wanted out of life. I mean, I joined because it looked cool, and I didn't have anything better to do. I was pretty much a late bloomer on all fronts. I didn't even realize I was gay until right before I left home. And then, after boot camp with Nguyen and getting assigned to the Barack with Vaughn and Hanson, I just started to feel so isolated, so cut off from everyone else. When I found out Robby knew, that now there were two people I could just totally be myself with? It was so exciting. And then I got selfish. But you're right: there's no excuse for what I've done. My actions. That's what I was ashamed of. And going just seemed like the best way to fix all of my problems in one stroke."

"And did it work? Did you fix it?"

"My life here is good, Lyta, better than I could have ever hoped. And yet, I almost died; I was so close to death that I could hear my ancestors singing Kikuyu burial songs for me from the spirit world. And you know I never bought into my grandmother's old religion. The point is, it really helped me see that my life has turned around dramatically. Then I heard you were coming here, and I was reminded of the mess I left, and how I didn't really try to fix anything. Not really. I was ashamed all over again."

"And then yesterday happened."

"My XO tries to murder the admiral, possibly you too. My boyfriend almost gets blown away. Lots of people died, including someone who was very special to a good friend of mine. Probably the worst day any of us has seen yet."

"And yet, despite all that, I really am glad to see you," she said.

"Me too. So you haven't been secretly plotting your revenge against me since the moment I left?"

"Of course not. Don't be so melodramatic. This isn't *Infinite Horizons*. I'm not going to slap you, or reveal that I tampered with your game console's interface so that you've now got exactly thirty seconds to live before a micro-pulse causes you to suffer a massive stroke and drop dead."

Blackwelder involuntarily glanced down at the 3-D sensor gloves he'd sat on the small table beside his chair. "That was a great episode," he said, slouching back into the seat. "We must have watched that one four or five times."

"At least." She paused. One by one, people shuffled past where they sat on their way to some other evening activity. "Robby really missed you too. Quite a bit more than I originally realized."

"But you figured it out, eventually."

"Actually, he told me."

"And you married him anyway," Blackwelder said, pointing to the silver band on her ring finger.

"He's changed. He doesn't laugh as much as he used to. He takes everything more seriously now. He has to; after all that flight simulator cross training, he's finally been promoted to an air group. But that's only part of it. He still has his fun side, for sure, but he treats everything and everyone more delicately. As if he knows what it feels like to lose something very important. So when he came into my quarters one night, tears streaming down his face, and he fell to his knees in front of me, I knew whatever he was about to say was real.

"He told me everything," she continued, "which, if I'm being honest, wasn't that great of a surprise. I think I had suspected as much, ever since that raid on the Elumerian starship. I could see it in your eyes when you looked at each other. He told me he loved you. That it hadn't been just some meaningless mistake, but that he actually had feelings for you. Strangely, that made me feel better. Like he wouldn't have endangered what we had over just a fling. He begged my forgiveness. He said you were the only man he's ever loved, and that I was the only woman he's ever loved, and that after me, he'd never love anyone again. It felt like he was honestly baring his soul to me. I know that sounds ridiculous, really, but I believed him. So I married him."

"Huh. He finally admits he loved me, but only to prove he loves you more. Typical Robby."

A pair of civilians near the front finished their game of chess. Once they left, Blackwelder and Abernathy were alone in the commons. The lights in the room dimmed, except for those directly above them, which cast a slanted halo over their armchairs.

"I'm happy for you both. Truly," he said.

"Thank you." She smiled, and for the first time since they'd started talking, Blackwelder felt at ease with his friend. "And you're happy?"

"I am," Blackwelder said, his face brightening. "His name is Juan Miguel, and he...I..." He trailed off.

"I know the feeling."

"So, Captain."

"Yes, Warrant Officer?"

"Why *did* my XO try to murder the admiral?"

"Probably because of what we came here to tell your general: the silent years are over. Without a doubt, war is coming to Fort Felix."

Chapter Eleven: Drums of War

"AND HE HASN'T said anything?" Blackwelder asked.

"Not a single word," Abernathy said. "He's made good on his promise."

Blackwelder and Abernathy stood outside Page's cell. It was the first time Blackwelder had ever been to H-Dome, the personal province of Fort Felix's Military Police. Arthur Page, stripped of his rank and labeled a traitor, sat chained to a chair behind a wall of clear laser-proof glass. There was a sheet and a dingy pillow flung in one of the corners, though Blackwelder wasn't sure when the last time Page had been allowed to use them. Page's eyes were dark and heavily ringed, not to mention his bruised cheek and still-bleeding lip. He stared maliciously at Abernathy, occasionally sparing Blackwelder a sideways glance. He wore a gray jumpsuit that was soaking wet and stained with blood.

This Arthur Page generated none of the authority he possessed while in the uniform and, instead, exuded a cold, calculating aura Blackwelder imagined was most common among serial killers. He wasn't afraid to be in such close proximity to Page, but Blackwelder was certainly not upset about the presence of the two armed MPs at either end of the cell.

Blackwelder gave Page another up-and-down glance. He frowned. "I see you've had him 'interrogated.'"

"Every version at our disposal, yes, but not on my order. Admiral Vaughn apparently takes attempts on his life very seriously."

The double doors behind Blackwelder swung open, and two men walked in: Juan Miguel, smartly dressed in a dark suit, and another man who was about four or five inches shorter with a severe brow. He wore a blue-gray coat with a shield on the breast that read Allied Earth Forces and Military Police wrapped around the Allied Earth globe. On his left shoulder, there was a red-and-gold patch that read Fort Felix Provost Marshal Office and Criminal Investigation Division.

"Captain Abernathy," Juan Miguel said, extending his hand.

She took it. "Ambassador Arías, good to see you again."

"Warrant Officer," Juan Miguel said.

"Ambassador," Blackwelder said with a serious nod. Any other time, he would have defaulted to flirting, but after what Page had done, it would be terribly inappropriate.

"This is Special Agent Nseir, our CID Chief. We've just come from a very interesting call with my friend General Shah on Mars."

"Is that so?" Abernathy asked.

Nseir smiled mischievously. "Oh yeah. Our caged bird here hasn't wanted to sing for us, unfortunately, but his silence has bought his cause nothing. General Shah has just apprehended a Retribution agent attempting to suicide-bomb the Mars base. Turns out," Nseir said as he walked up to the glass of Page's cell, "he doesn't possess your resolve."

"The traitor indicated that the Retribution know about the imminent Elumerian attack. They activated sleepers to sabotage strategic points in the Allied Earth defenses," Juan Miguel said.

"What's your game, Mam?" Nseir said, tapping on the glass like a small child at an aquarium. "Do you and your traitorous cult *want* to see the Earth destroyed?"

"Special Agent," Juan Miguel admonished. In response, Nseir backed away from Page's cell wall but didn't take his eyes away from the prisoner.

Abernathy looked suspiciously between Juan Miguel and Nseir. "*Mam?*"

"Yeah. Man-Against-Man. It's sort of a nickname from back in the European Union that we gave these anarchist dogs who want us to go back to fighting each other, instead of the real enemy out there."

"Hmph," She very coolly turned and exited through the double doors. Blackwelder eyed Juan Miguel, who seemed confused by the exchange, and then Nseir, who appeared to have interpreted Abernathy's meaning just fine. They followed her out, Blackwelder stealing one last look at the captive Page before nodding to the guards and pushing past the doors.

In the hallway, Abernathy was several feet away at the guard station, retrieving her weapon. They'd all had to surrender them in order to enter the antechamber to Page's cell. The guard station was backed up against one of the walls of this eight-sided room; six of the other paths led to different maximum-security cells, and the seventh path led back to H-Dome's main corridor.

Nseir approached Abernathy and the guard station with measured steps, but stopped just close enough to conduct his own business. "Did I miss something, Captain?" He waved his palm over a sensor on the desk and a secret compartment opened, revealing a short-barreled laser gun. Nseir snatched it up and stuck it in his holster.

Blackwelder followed suit, walking over to the desk and waving his hand. He retrieved his L9 and made eye contact with Juan Miguel. He too looked concerned about the scene they expected was about to unfold.

"So, *Special Agent*," she said, ignoring his question and refusing to face him. "I take it you're a civilian, then?"

"I am. Do you take issue with that?"

"Not at all. Just curious about what would bring someone from the EU—someone like you—all the way out here. Ambassador Arías is a representative of the senate, so that's one thing. But a CID chief?"

"Yeah, I'm a CID chief. My father was Operations Director for the Bureau of International Investigations, and my grandfather was Chief Inspector to His Majesty the King of Western Europe. What exactly is your point?"

"No point. I'm sure you worked very hard to get appointed to a military command. How lucky we are to have you here on base," she said, finally turning toward him. "In fact, given your experience with these 'Mams' and the general caliber of EU folk, I imagine none among us could more easily slip into the midset of a Retribution traitor."

Nseir's eyes grew large and his lips tightened. The color drained from his face. "Are you actually suggesting that—"

A voice emanating from Juan Miguel's wrist cut across Nseir. "Ambassador Arías, General Kilmer would like to see you and Captain Abernathy in his office, please." Juan Miguel slid his fingers along his forearm toward his wrist, and the face of the general's assistant appeared.

"Of course." He nodded to Abernathy.

Abernathy cocked a smile at Nseir. "Special Agent." She touched Juan Miguel on the shoulder and led him out of the octagon without a backward glance.

Blackwelder let the awkward silence sit for a moment before saying, "Well, I'm going to go check on the reinforcements." Sensing that Nseir had no intention of responding, Blackwelder finally took his leave.

Blackwelder arrived at J-Dome in time to see a large squad exit the weapons training simulator. His area was seeing a nearly constant stream of men and women ever since the ground reinforcements had started arriving the week prior. Per Lt. Col. Lee's orders, Blackwelder and Greene had been working double shifts, trying to get the new additions acclimated to Triton and ready for battle.

The door to the Arena opened, and Greene emerged with a weary, disgruntled-looking crew. Given their need, they were programming the Arena to help provide training for larger groups using high-impact scenarios but for lengths of time more like the other simulators rather than the normal six-day mission. In fact, no one had attempted a true Arena run since Brant Squad's near-tragic debacle. Most still blamed the incident on faulty equipment, not on sabotage, and so presumably would do anything to avoid being locked inside a 3-D holographic death trap. Greene joined Blackwelder at the center console station while the squad headed straight for the exit.

"Warrant Officer," Greene said stiffly.

"Second Lieutenant." While Blackwelder acknowledged that Page's actions had cleared Greene of complicity in the Arena incident, it had done nothing to improve the overall standing of their interactions.

"I just finished field maneuvers with the reinforcements from the Malia. You're up for the monkeys from Solara-Pluto." Greene pulled a hand towel from his belt and mopped his sweaty brow.

"The last of their unit is still going through medical screenings for environmental fitness. I'd rather put them through their paces all at once, instead of splitting them into arbitrary groups."

"We're sort of preparing for a war here. Not sure your personal preference is the most important thing to consider here."

"It's not about that. It's about their cohesion as a team," Blackwelder said, rounding on Greene. "They train together, they learn to work together, and they learn they can depend on each other. Having each other's backs is what will keep them alive." Blackwelder held his stare against Greene a couple moments too long to maintain subtlety.

"You got something to say, Blackwelder?"

"I think I've made myself perfectly clear. *Sir.*"

"Officers," Burton said. Blackwelder hadn't noticed her approach. Normally a stickler for formality, she would have saluted them both, but in the days since the bombing, Blackwelder noticed she'd adhered to the strictures of authority less and less.

He considered his words for a moment, but decided straight forward was the best course. "Burton... How—how are you?"

"Perfectly well, Warrant Officer. Was that the detail from the AES Malia that just finished training?"

"Yeah," Greene said, swiping his brow again. "And as the one of us who's on schedule, I will be at the Deck until my next shift." And with that, he exited.

Blackwelder turned back to Burton, not wanting to let the subject drop. "Really, how are you holding—"

"Lieutenant Colonel Lee sent me for an update on the training progress. Are you off schedule?"

"No." Blackwelder turned back to the console. "My training with the AEB Solara-Pluto recruits will start within the hour, Sergeant Major."

"Good." She turned to leave. "Keep an eye out while you're running them," she added. "I'm not entirely sure we can trust them."

"Why not?"

"There was a glitch in the system while we were running background scans on a couple of them. We've triple-checked and they've all been cleared, but it's too suspicious to ignore."

"Noted."

As she left J-Dome, De Silva and Bonner walked in. Blackwelder had tapped them as his training assistants for the day since De Silva acted like he was in charge anyway, and Bonner could use the extra practice.

"Who died and made her XO?" De Silva said. He and Bonner both laughed, but their faces blanched when they realized Blackwelder was standing well within earshot.

"Sorry, sir," they both mumbled.

"Get to M-Dome and get the last of the Solara-Pluto dusties here. Now!"

"Yes, sir!" they said, scattering like insects from a sudden burst of light.

BLACKWELDER PACED FIFTEEN feet away from the staircase that led up to Fort Felix's Command Headquarters. It wasn't that he wasn't allowed to enter the HQ, per se; he simply had no legitimate reason to be there. At least, he didn't think needing to see his boyfriend would be acceptable. And with the base on high alert and everyone still reeling from Page's betrayal, Blackwelder thought it wise not to give the determined-looking MPs guarding the entryway a reason to shoot first. Four guards stood firm on either side of the glass-and-steel grand staircase, the only objects in the busy corridor not moving, as foot traffic mostly bent around them toward I-Dome, the civilian quarters, and M-Dome, the hospital wing. The only other traffic there in A-Dome were those moving off toward Blackwelder's left, heading to specific offices. They, of course, had special pass codes embedded in their com devices that would allow them to walk through the automated security scanners.

And so, Blackwelder continued to pace across the face of Fort Felix's emblem—nine white stars arched above a three-pronged pitchfork—as he waited, trying not to appear too conspicuous.

"Spencer," Juan Miguel called as he quickly descended the stairs. "Sorry, that last briefing ran over. We've been stuck on the Floor for hours." He moved past the guards and walked to Blackwelder. "I hear you've been keeping busy."

"The ground reinforcements that Vaughn called in? Yeah, I run them through target practice; Greene runs them through combat training. It's been a fairly constant cycle since they started arriving."

"Everyone will be warmed up then. When things get interesting."

"I think they're mostly trying to keep us distracted. It's been over five years since the last shot was fired. Most of us didn't even enlist until after Crescent Moon. They laugh and joke, but they're...*we're* scared as hell; none of us have any idea what to expect. The only person who does—"

"Burton?" Juan Miguel said.

"She's hurting, but I can't get to her. I just hope she holds it together and doesn't do anything crazy."

"Like what?"

"Like walk into the brig and shoot Page in the face. I get the sense that nothing would give her more satisfaction."

"She's strong-willed, but she's got an even stronger sense of honor. She'll do the right thing."

"Yeah, but according to whom?" Blackwelder said, trailing off. "So, you've gotten to spend a lot of time with Lyta."

"She's great. So clever. I love the way she handles Admiral Vaughn without him even realizing it. I see why you like her."

"You two talking a lot about me?"

"Every chance we get, obviously. Not much else going on."

Blackwelder pulled Juan Miguel in close. The middle prong of Triton's staff pointed to the center-most star, the width of which was all the distance that separated the two of them. Their lips were on a collision course until Juan Miguel's touch-com sounded.

"Ambassador," said General Kilmer, "we need you back on the Floor."

Blackwelder sighed as Juan Miguel pulled away.

"I'll be right there, General." He turned to leave. "Coming?"

"I...sure." He figured they'd be under fire at any moment; now was as good a time to go sightseeing as any.

They walked past the guards who took turns visually scrutinizing Blackwelder as his boots clopped against the steel steps. At the top of the stairs, a door that bore the same emblem as the floor below pulled open to reveal the Command HQ.

It was a curious room. Solid blue and black square tiles stretched along the walls and crawled across the floor. Whitish desks and chairs stood out in sharp relief, stationed at intervals throughout the room. From where they'd entered, HQ resembled a mini sports stadium. Soldiers toiled at anonymous tasks in the bleachers, while a gently sloping stairway led to the room's valley, the Floor. Bright lights pointed expectantly in the direction of the small plateau. Seven identical view screens formed a semicircle, images flashing across each that seemed to keep the men and women in the square, beige workstations at the four corners of the Floor quite busy. And in the center, around an Arthurian round table, stood Admiral Vaughn, General Kilmer, Colonel Tsui, and Captain Macke-Abernathy, as it was written on her uniform. Vaughn looked up as they entered.

Juan Miguel nodded to Blackwelder and paused, and Blackwelder correctly took that to mean he was to stay there in the stands. Even as the official representative of the senate, Blackwelder knew his partner's cachet only extended so far. Juan Miguel made his way down the aisle to join the others at the Floor.

"I wasn't aware that your warrant officer had been promoted to your intelligence detail, General," Vaughn said.

"He hasn't. He's with me," Juan Miguel said before the question was allowed to linger.

"Yes. We know," Vaughn said.

"You'll have to excuse my son, Admiral," Senator Arías said. His face was displayed prominently on one of the seven screens. "He seems constantly in want of discretionary judgment."

"Gentlemen, let's focus on the matter at hand," Kilmer said, cutting across Juan Miguel. Even from where he was standing, Blackwelder could see Juan Miguel's posture shift as he prepared to respond.

So this was Juan Miguel's father, the man who had so callously banished his son from the world. His head seemed small. Blackwelder was unimpressed.

"You had a question, Senator?" General Kilmer asked.

"Yes, yes. The Tridecagon would like a report on our battle-readiness."

"As it happens, Senator, Warrant Officer Blackwelder was just informing me that the Weapons Training Battalion is working constantly with the reinforcements to ensure that they are primed for action."

"We're on high alert, Senator. Every man and woman on this base, military and civilian, is taking their training and preparation very seriously. We'll be ready," the general said.

"Well, it's good to hear, General. The people of Allied Earth—" the senator began.

"Apologies, Admiral, but there is an emergency transmission from the AES Keqiang," the communications officer said.

"On screen," said Vaughn. A woman's face appeared on the screen next to Senator Arías. "Commander Dawson, you have news?"

"Admiral, long-range scanners in Solara-Pluto are registering a significant electro-magnetic disturbance, the type consistent with wormhole activity. We think it's them, sir," she said seriously.

Just then, the room was thrown into complete darkness, but only for a hair's breadth; the outline of the blue panels in the walls lit up first, and then, as if to dramatically draw attention to the main event, the other lights reasserted themselves in a gentle wave from the nosebleeds to the Floor. Before Blackwelder could fully take stock, the situation seemed to have righted itself.

"EM shields holding, sir," an HQ staffer told General Kilmer.

The screen next to Commander Dawson's face showed a satellite view of Triton. Fort Felix was just distinguishable from the surface of the moon, and Vaughn's four Allied Earth ships had taken up positions.

Despite the fact that black emptiness occupied the space between the ships and the moon, the image began to shimmer and a distortion field became visible even as the other monitors snowed over and the lights dimmed slightly.

"Dear God," Senator Arías said. They all watched as the epicenter of the distortion field ripped in half and collapsed into itself. A wormhole appeared, and emerging slowly from it were giant, bulbous spacecrafts shaped oddly like whales. Blackwelder recognized them immediately. Moments after it had appeared, the wormhole closed and vanished, and in its wake were fully functional Elumerian starships. There were four to match the Allied Earth vessels, but each was one and a half times the size of its human counterpart.

And then, a siren blared.

"What now?" the senator whined.

"Internal security breach, sir," said one of the staffers. "It's coming from H-Dome, the brig."

Juan Miguel looked straight up at Blackwelder. "Page," they said in unison.

"Colonel, get a squad—" General Kilmer began.

"Sir! Their weapons are powering up. They're preparing to fire on the ships!" said Commander Dawson.

Blackwelder stared at the faces of every single one of the people standing at the round table, as they in turn looked at each other. Even from where he stood, he could see the flicker of desperation in their eyes, as he presumed none of them wanted to give the order that would cast them all headlong into war. But desperation faded as reality set in, turning to inevitability; the war had already begun.

Vaughn pounded his fist onto the table. "Open fire!"

Chapter Twelve: Gods of the Sea

FORT FELIX'S SURFACE-TO-AIR gun turrets whirred to life and aimed for the darkness of space. The view screens in the Command HQ lit up as the deadly space battle raged; the Allied Earth warships' energy bursts exploded against the empty space surrounding the Elumerian vessels. Their shields held. The Elumerians returned fire, three of the ships blasting the humans' starships while the fourth concentrated a steady green ray against the military installation on the surface of Triton. Their shields held as well.

"Blackwelder, get down to the brig," Kilmer said.

"Brant Squad is on it, sir." Blackwelder turned to leave.

"Be careful," Juan Miguel said, only slightly inclining his head in Blackwelder's direction. His tone wasn't emotional or imploring; it was stern, matter-of-fact, as if it were an order he expected him to carry out, no different from the one the general had issued. Blackwelder smiled and nodded as he exited the HQ.

DE SILVA, BONNER, PETREY, Bailey, and Chiu activated their weapons, switching off their safeties. In no time, they'd assembled with Blackwelder outside of the brig. He looked them each in the eye as he loaded the lethal laser cartridge into his L9. The time for simulations had passed. He was about to say as much when he saw Burton approaching them.

"Sergeant Major, what are you doing here? Shouldn't you be assisting Lieutenant Colonel Lee?"

"You called for Brant Squad. I am a member of Brant Squad," she said as she readied her own weapon.

"You have other responsibilities, Burton. I'm sure the lieutenant colonel—" Blackwelder began.

"I am a member of Brant Squad," she said firmly. "I am here to support my team."

Blackwelder knew that wasn't the only reason she was there: Arthur Page was certainly somehow involved, and Burton had a score to settle. But she had more active duty experience than all of them combined, and Blackwelder knew how foolish it would be to try to cut her out.

He nodded. "On me, Brant Squad. We're going in hot. Weapons ready."

Burton and the rest of the squad flanked Blackwelder. As the doors to the brig slid open, Brant Squad pushed in. Several bodies lay near the entrance, including the guards who had been posted at the weapons check. Errant laser fire marked the walls of the eight-sided room; the aggressors had won, but they hadn't been very precise about it. Blackwelder couldn't tell if that would work to their advantage or not.

They carefully approached Page's cell, and just as Blackwelder had feared, it was empty. The two MPs who had been standing guard were also dead, along with a couple other members of Fort Felix's security. Barely stirring next to them was Special Agent Nseir.

Blackwelder rushed over. "Nseir. What happened?" He dropped down to Nseir's side.

"They came for him. Caught us all by surprise." He was clutching his abdomen as blood spilled freely between his fingers.

"Bonner!"

"Medics are already on their way, sir," she replied as she tapped away at her touch-com. Then, she dropped to one knee and pulled a small syringe from a bag in her pack, injecting Nseir. "This should slow the bleeding, but won't do much for the pain."

Chiu stood up and waved Bonner over. "We got another live one over here, Bonner." She jumped to her feet and hurried over.

"It was the Malia recruits; I could tell from their uniform patches," Nseir breathed heavily to Blackwelder. "They've been infiltrated by the Retribution."

Blackwelder glanced up at Burton, remembering what she'd said.

Nseir coughed, and a small trail of blood slid out of the crook in his mouth. "Well, at least this'll make your captain friend happy."

Blackwelder's attention snapped back. "What do you mean?"

"Me almost breathing my last. Blasted by my own, eh? I feel like she would have shot me herself if she thought she could prove something."

"Abernathy? No, that wasn't about you," Blackwelder said. "Her father... I remember her saying he was from the EU, and he worked in law enforcement, like you. He made her life very...difficult. But she would never wish you harm. Just hang tight; the medics will be here in about a minute."

There was a deafening boom. The walls shook and Blackwelder looked up, knowing it had something to do with the Elumerian ship firing down on them. "Petrey, report."

Petrey slid his fingers along his forearm to activate his com screen. "Sir, it looks like...one of the four shield generators for the base just went offline. Shields down to sixty percent overall. The Barack and the Keqiang have launched Cam fighters in response."

An alarm blared to life, echoing down the corridors of the entire base. Emergency lighting flashed as all of Brant Squad looked around, confused.

"This is General Kilmer. The main hangar bay has been breached. Repeat, the main hangar bay has been breached. Elumerians have entered the base. All hands converge on D-Dome and take these Fish Faces out!"

De Silva's face blanched. "This is happening."

For a moment, Blackwelder wasn't sure if De Silva would pass out, run for the nearest exit, or drop down and curl into the fetal position.

Finally, De Silva said, "Sir, we need to get over there!"

"Sir!" Petrey yelled before Blackwelder could react. "On the screen!" Petrey pointed to a small view screen on a wall next to the access point for the L-Dome corridor, the only dome aside from Central Command HQ that was attached to their current location in H-Dome.

As Blackwelder and Brant Squad watched the screen, they saw the rogue Malia recruits in all-black uniforms locked in a firefight with the soldiers in the beta hangar, essentially the back door to Fort Felix.

"He's trying to escape Triton," Bonner said, but Blackwelder didn't get the impression that Page was the type to flee; he seemed too resolute, too intent on completing his mission, whatever that was, to simply run away.

"Or give the Elumerians another point of entry," Chiu said. More likely. But Page had been methodical in his planning. What was the specific advantage of taking the beta hangar, as opposed to any other dome? Blackwelder's mind raced as he visualized the base's map. He looked at Burton, and then, it clicked.

"Engineering. He's going to try to get to Engineering from L-Dome."

"He could take out all of the base's defenses from there," Burton said. "The Elumerians wouldn't need to come after us dome by dome; they could wipe us all out from the sky."

"Do you really think that's his plan, sir?" Petrey asked.

"It's the best way to cause the most damage. Losing Fort Felix tonight would be a crushing blow to Allied Earth."

De Silva pondered it; something didn't appear to be adding up for him. "But L and K don't connect. To get to Engineering from the beta hangar, he'd have to go *outside*."

Burton pointed toward the hangar. "There are maintenance ATVs in the hangar. He gets one of those, and it's a short ride to K-Dome."

"We've got to stop him. Right now."

"But what about Nseir and the other survivors?" Bonner asked. "The breach will slow down the medics en route."

"Go," Nseir said. He weakly pulled a laser rifle from one of the dead MPs toward him. "I'll hold this down until help arrives."

Blackwelder could see that Nseir was barely viable, let alone capable of mounting any sort of defense. "You can't even stand up."

"Don't worry about me, I got it. Just get out of here!" Blackwelder gave Nseir a solemn nod, which he reciprocated.

"All right. Let's move!" Blackwelder led his squad into the L-Dome corridor. He activated his touch-com view screen. "Blackwelder to HQ, come in."

"Go ahead, Blackwelder," General Kilmer said.

"Sir, Page shot his way out of the brig with Retribution agents from the Malia. All other brig personnel are down, save Special Agent Nseir, who is awaiting medical support. We believe Page is heading to Engineering to disable the base defenses. Brant Squad is in pursuit."

"Don't let him succeed, son. You stop him, whatever it takes. Understood?"

"Understood, sir," Blackwelder said. Burton tried to hide a mirthless grin at overhearing the order; she'd have her revenge after all.

JUAN MIGUEL NODDED as the last of the communication came across his private channel. "General, I- and E-Domes are locked down and sealed. The civilians are secured in their quarters. MPs are posted out front, and Postmaster Zeng has assumed local command and armed a small troop posted inside the domes."

"Thank you, Ambassador," Kilmer said. He kept his eyes fixed on one of the screens displaying a barrage of laser fire between Allied Earth warships and the Elumerian threat.

"Shouldn't you be with them, Ambassador?" Vaughn asked. The room went suddenly quiet as people stopped typing or switched from full voice to whispers. "Now that they've brought the fight to us, you should be secured. Part of the reason we reinforce civilian quarters is for political assets, such as you. I can have one of my men escort you."

Juan Miguel glanced at General Kilmer, who as usual betrayed no sign of a response.

"I am exactly where I'm supposed to be, Admiral Vaughn. But your concern for my well-being has been noted."

"Admiral!" Abernathy said, cutting across them. "The primary enemy ship has turned its ground weapon against the Barack. She's taking heavy damage!"

On-screen, the green beam that had been previously directed at Fort Felix was now blasting away at the Barack. The warship's shield seemed to be holding, but by the readings coming in at the bottom of the screen, it was obvious they wouldn't for too much longer.

Vaughn pounded the console. "Get Hanson on the line."

Hanson appeared on one of the seven screens. Though they had not been formally introduced, Juan Miguel recognized Colonel Hanson as Blackwelder's former XO while he was stationed on the Barack. "Admiral, we're diverting all available power to the shields. We'll hold it off as long as we can,"

"Incoming from Captain Macke," the communications officer said.

"On screen," Vaughn said. An image of Robby Macke in a flight suit appeared on one of the screens. He was seated in what looked like a cramped cockpit. Again, Juan Miguel had never met Macke, but he'd of course taken some time to look him up.

"Admiral, sir, this is Macke. Theta Squadron is away. All fighters engaging the mantas!"

On screen, the last team of Cams pulled to the front of the Barack and immediately dove into the battle. Each of the fighters had the Greek letter painted on their wings, and Macke's Theta was in red. Theta Squadron held a tight X-shaped formation and cut a wide path down the middle of an advancing guard of manta ships that pitched up and down on their approach as if they were riding ocean currents. As some of the enemy ships scattered, Theta Squadron rounded for a second-wave attack.

Vaughn nodded. "Keep it up, Captain."

"I want all surface weapons targeted on the primary starship," Kilmer said. "We'll just have to hope we were able to launch enough air support before the main hangar was breached."

"Sir," Colonel Tsui said solemnly, her eyebrows arched high, "we've lost the main hangar. The Elumerians have entered B-Dome."

"Then we hold them in B-Dome. If we don't, they'll have the run of the entire base."

BRANT SQUAD EMERGED from the corridor between the brig and the beta hangar, weapons firing. With just a nod from Blackwelder, the squad split into two, one half taking cover behind one of the computer consoles, the other behind a gutted Cam fighter that had been in process of being repaired. Most of their fire was wasted; L-Dome was set up similarly to the main hangar bay in D-Dome, but was only half the size and had many more recessed spaces for vehicle and part storage, giving Page and his men ample cover. Their initial attack did however have an upswing, in that it provided cover for the few surviving soldiers to fall in behind Brant Squad.

"Shin, you're alive!" Petrey clapped the man on the back. "When everything started going down, I didn't know if you were in here or the main hangar."

"Yeah, I'm alive. Barely. And mostly thanks to you guys. Another minute and the rest of us would be dead too," Shin said. Half of his face and uniform were covered in soot and he had multiple cuts down his neck. From the look of him, Blackwelder surmised that Shin had narrowly escaped an explosion.

"Shin, is it? Sit-rep," Blackwelder said, as the rest of the squad continued to exchange fire.

"Sir, we'd just gotten the order from HQ to start securing the hangar when these *asshairs* came in shooting. They got our lieutenant right off, then took out the communications. I tried to use my touch-com, but they must have our frequency because they activated a local jammer."

Blackwelder nodded in acknowledgement. He peered around the Cam to get a better look: he could make out twelve targets, including Page. Three were loading up ATVs. Two more were pulling suits for the trip. They were pretty well covered, and most people seemed to be distracted by the otherwise pointless shooting taking place, but Blackwelder had a shot.

With surgical precision, Blackwelder loosed two quick blasts from his L9 and caught the two men collecting space suits in the back of the head. The bodies and suits hit the ground with a heavy thud, which caught the attention of all the Retribution agents.

"Did he just..." Shin began, looking at Blackwelder with a mix of awe and terror.

"Yup," Petrey said.

"Blackwelder!" Page yelled from behind one of the girders. "Only you could nail a hit like that. You really are one of the best shots I've seen in my entire career."

"And which career is that, Page? As a respected Allied Earth military officer? Or a heartless, psychopathic Retribution traitor?" Blackwelder said. He kept his gun at the ready. If Page gave him so much as half an inch, he would end him.

"Sorry, son. This isn't the part where I tell you my life story. My men and I are on a tight schedule. But I will give you this one chance to save your squad. Put your weapons down and walk away."

"So you can kill us later? Or leave us for the Fish Faces? I don't think so!" De Silva blurted.

Blackwelder spared an instant's glance at De Silva. Being with the other half of the squad, he was beyond Blackwelder's immediate reach, and now wasn't the time. Besides, De Silva *was* standing next to Burton, and even in the fraction of time he turned his attention, Blackwelder could already see De Silva withering under her gaze.

"The mouth on that one," Page said. "How can you stand it?"

"De Silva is eager, but his sentiment is correct. We're not letting you walk out of here," Blackwelder said.

"Then I suppose you will die trying to stop us!"

On cue, one of Page's men stepped into the open with a grenade launcher. Blackwelder made a quick adjustment, shifting his aim slightly to his left. One blast to the head, and Blackwelder killed the man dead. But the dead man had already squeezed his trigger.

"Get down!" Blackwelder yelled as he shoved everyone around him to the ground. The explosion tore the fighter Blackwelder had been hiding behind into pieces and sent them hurtling toward the back wall. They were only just able to clear the debris' path, as one of the pieces lightly grazed Blackwelder's back as it flew overhead.

Just then, two large metal doors ground into place, creating a barrier between Brant Squad and the Retribution.

Burton struggled to get back to her feet. "They're opening the airlock!"

"We were right about their plan. Shut it down."

Burton ran over to the nearest console, but the sequences she was entering seemed to have no effect.

"He's locked in some sort of override. I can't get control back!"

Blackwelder staggered over to the metal doors. Through a small window, he was able to peer into the other side: Page and his men exited the exterior door onto Triton's surface. They rode on three ATVs, each vehicle seating three people, their numbers now down to nine. The exterior doors stayed open, though, which prevented the dome from automatically restoring pressure.

"Bailey, Chiu, get that exterior door closed so we can get this opened, now," Blackwelder said. They ran over to the panel where the airlock doors met the wall and started to work.

"Shin, how many ATVs are in here?"

"We keep four fueled and ready to go, sir."

"They just made off with three of them." Blackwelder paused. "Okay, De Silva, Chiu, you're with me. We'll take the last ATV and pursue. The rest of you, head back to base and try to come at Engineering from the other side—"

"I'm coming with you," Burton said.

"No, I need someone to lead the squad—"

"Then send De Silva, sir. If you're planning to go in there three against nine, you're going to need more practiced hands." He wanted to argue, to say that Burton only wanted in so she could take the final shot herself, but it was impossible to disagree with her logic.

"Exterior doors closed, sir," Chiu said.

"Interior doors open in ten seconds," Bailey added.

Blackwelder nodded his approval to Burton. "I doubt they'll be able to come to you, so Shin, you all need to get yourselves to medical."

"Sir," Shin said.

"De Silva, you've got the home team. Double back and get over to Engineering ASAP."

"Yes, sir." De Silva frowned. He was obviously disappointed but, after his previous outburst, seemed to think better than to argue.

The gears on the inner metal doors whirred to life and pulled apart.

"Alright, people, you've got your orders. Let's mov—" Blackwelder began. As the way became clear, he could see that Page had left him a gift: the last ATV, its engine compartment charred, its tires flattened.

"Dammit," Blackwelder said. "Alright, new plan: everyone suit up."

HUMAN SPACE FIGHTERS clashed with the Elumerians' manta ships in a chaotic array that reminded Juan Miguel of one of those antique video games. It seemed absolutely absurd to him—the four giant birds facing off on either side of an invisible line drawn in the darkness, the tiny bees buzzing all around them—until he remembered that every flash of an explosion meant another life had left the universe forever. Death, the only tangible result of war.

"They're evacuating," Abernathy said. She pointed to a screen next to the one Juan Miguel had been contemplating. All around the edges, the screen showed what looked like quickly declining vital signs for the Barack. Little silver pods began exiting from the rear of the ship, but they were quickly drawing the attention of the Elumerian mantas.

"They've spotted them. Those pods will never make it here!" Juan Miguel said.

"You're right," Abernathy said. She tapped her touch-com. "Macke, the escape pods are defenseless!"

"Theta Squadron: cover the pods!"

Macke's crew peeled off from the larger fight and flew around the Barack to where the pods were attempting to reach Triton. On the screen, Theta Squadron formed its X-pattern again, only this time one of the tips was missing; it looked like Macke had lost one of his fighters. Macke pushed his Cam into a hard dive toward the pods, then pulled up at the last minute, which brought him and the squadron into the mantas' direct line of fire. Unprepared for the maneuver, though, several manta ships were destroyed as Theta Squadron opened fire. More mantas attempted to back up the initial attack, but Theta held its defensive position, effectively shielding the evacuation.

Though he didn't really want to admit, Juan Miguel was impressed.

"Hanson, report," said Vaughn.

Hanson appeared on the screen, somber and resolute. His face had an ashen, gray quality to it, but when he spoke, his voice was unwavering and caught everyone's attention.

"Admiral Vaughn, the Barack has sustained an irreversible amount of damage. The warp core is intact, but the engines are shot. The bridge deflector shields are down to seven percent, and we've already lost decks three and six. We've evacuated ninety percent of the ship to a safe distance from the conflict zone on Triton."

"Fall back to Saturn, Colonel," Vaughn said. "She's seen enough battle for today."

"She won't make it, sir. As I mentioned, the core is intact, but the rest of her—if we attempt long-range travel, the Barack will be torn apart, and it will have been for nothing. At least this way, we can take out their main starship."

"This way, Colonel?" Vaughn asked. He looked nervously at General Kilmer. Juan Miguel turned to Abernathy. He could tell from the look in her eye that they both understood perfectly the colonel's meaning.

"It's been an honor serving with you, Admiral Vaughn," Hanson said, right before the screen went black and the line fell silent.

All eyes in the HQ turned toward the screens: the Barack began firing all of its weapons, all trained on the primary Elumerian starship. Using impulse engine power, the warship slowly rotated its position and inched toward the alien vessel in a perpendicular fashion. The manta ships must have suspected what was about to happen, because they abandoned their pursuit of the smaller aircraft and focused their attacks on the Barack. The starship itself must have realized it too, as its engines warmed up.

"All hands, focus all your fire on that lead ship! Fighters, box them in; they only need a couple of minutes," Vaughn said.

The fighters not already caught in deadly skirmishes close to the moon's surface turned their attention toward the lead Elumerian ship. Even the other Allied Earth warships opened fire against it, which prompted the starships they'd been battling to turn their weapons against the Barack. All the while, the Barack moved closer, picking up speed as it swam through the vacuum.

"Their shields are gone!" Juan Miguel said. He and Abernathy had been watching the screens closely. As if in response, explosions peppered the surface of the Barack. The alien fleet managed to scatter the fighters buzzing around their flagship, but it was too late: the Barack, trailing pieces of itself like an old jalopy and visibly on fire, even from that distance, rammed into the side of the Elumerian vessel.

Juan Miguel's breath caught; for a brief, sickening moment, it appeared as if the Barack had crashed against an invisible barrier and would crumple into nothing, the Elumerians' ship a safe distance away on the other side. But then a bright flash and a ripple of light later, the Barack overwhelmed the enemy ship's shield capabilities, fully T-boning into its target. The Barack, already half-destroyed, erupted in a massive fireball that was quickly sucked inside the alien starship, and in a moment's time, both vehicles were utterly rent by the collision.

"WE'RE ONE KILOMETER away from K-Dome, sir," Bailey said.

"Keep moving!" Blackwelder shouted. He silently chided himself. Splitting the group in two would have been a terrible idea, as each fraction would have been hopelessly out-gunned. Their only hope at success lay in a show of the full squad's force and a lot of luck. Besides, Blackwelder had no idea what they'd encounter between the domes; moving quickly on an ATV would have been one thing, but since they had to make the trek on foot, seven stood a better chance of facing down whatever surprises might present themselves than three did.

Brant Squad ran across the surface of Triton, keeping their formation tight, the visual evidence of Page's ATV tracks never far from his line of sight. Ice crystals on the frozen ground crunched under their booted feet, their suits and their artificial gravity generators making running possible. The landscape was dotted with peaking crags of ice, some six or seven feet tall—at this distance, just enough to obscure Blackwelder's vision. Lights flashed sporadically above their heads as Elumerian mantas and Allied Earth Cams battled in the sky. And then, a flare of orange above them drew all their attention, and Brant Squad witnessed the final sacrifice of the AES Barack.

"Robby," Blackwelder whispered.

"Sir," De Silva shouted. He pointed to a position several hundred feet ahead of them. Just behind an ice ridge, smoke trailed into the sky as the subtle hues of laser fire reflected off the ice.

"Form up! And keep your eyes open. We don't know what's on the other side of that ridge," Blackwelder said.

Their ranks tightened up as they advanced together, cautiously, on the ridge. As they approached, the exchange became clearer, even through the distortion of Blackwelder's helmet. Slimming down to a single-file line, Blackwelder led Brant Squad to the back of the ridge, where his team's presence could remain concealed. After giving the signal to halt their progression, Blackwelder advanced on the ridge and peered around the side.

A human fighter pilot crouched behind her downed Cam. Blackwelder could make out black skid marks along the ice where she'd ground to a halt several feet in front of this ice ridge, a bold stroke of luck. Advancing steadily on her position were two distinct streams of laser fire, unevenly but predictably blasting against the wreckage. Blackwelder deduced their foes were two Elumerians on foot. The scene reminded him of the Arena, which sent a cold shiver down his spine, causing his back muscles to clench. He shook the feeling off.

"One Cam fighter down, taking fire from two approaching Elumerians," Blackwelder said to Burton back behind the ridge. "I'm going to move in to more closely assess. When I give the signal, you pour around this ridge, guns blazing."

Burton nodded. The rest of the squad gave Blackwelder solemn, serious looks.

"Allied Earth soldier," Blackwelder said, his body still mostly concealed in case the pilot decided to shoot first.

She spun around and trained her weapon on the origin of the voice.

Blackwelder was stunned. He recognized her immediately. She had the exact same face as his former squad mate Corporal DeFrank, except that was impossible; Corporal DeFrank was dead. This woman, whoever she was, was wearing a silver-starred lieutenant's bar next to her Cam fighter patch. He raised his hands in appeasement as he darted around the ridge and into the shadow of the downed Cam. The Elumerians, though still a distance away, continued to fire.

"DeFrank?" he asked shakily. She held her aim against him.

"I am, but I'm guessing not the one you're thinking of. Who are you?" she said, dodging sparks.

"Blackwelder. I used to be a member of Jinx Squad."

"You were on my sister's team. You were probably there wh—" she began but was cut off by more incoming laser blasts.

"My squad is just behind that ridge," he said, pointing behind him. "We're on our way to one of the exterior domes, but it looks like you could use some help."

"I could at that," DeFrank said, finally lowering her weapon.

Blackwelder raised his laser rifle and adjusted his scope; two Elumerians strode across the field of ice, firing as they crept closer to their position. They had arm-mounted energy shields that Blackwelder assumed had greatly bolstered their confidence in this brazen attack. The shields were only large enough to cover their torsos, though, leaving their legs and heads uncovered. In direct fire, they'd have to adjust the position of the shield to better protect their upper body, leaving even more of the lower body exposed. Blackwelder could work with that.

"On my mark, lay down suppressing fire from that side of the ship," Blackwelder said, pointing away from where they were standing. "It will slow them down just enough for my men to move in. Sir," he added hastily. He had always outranked Corporal DeFrank.

"Sounds like a good plan," DeFrank said. She took up her position.

"Mark," Blackwelder said. Immediately, he and DeFrank began to open fire. Her blasts generally bounced of their shields, but Blackwelder targeted the ground near their feet. As anticipated, the attack brought them to a standstill.

"Brant Squad! Now!" Blackwelder yelled.

Brant Squad split in two and poured around the sides of the ridge. Their steady, sudden fire surprised the Elumerians, who had to turn to use their shield to deflect the blasts coming from a wider angle than the previous attack. This gave Blackwelder exactly the opening he'd been waiting for. With two quick shots, he brought both alien soldiers down.

DeFrank turned to look at him. "Blackwelder. My sister mentioned you. I'm afraid she didn't do you justice."

"I've trained harder since I've known your sister. Hopefully I've gotten better. What happened here?"

"They clipped me and forced me down. And then, when they saw I'd survived, the arrogant bastards landed to finish me off in person."

"That means their ship's intact," Chiu said.

"Yes it does," DeFrank said, already starting to cross the battlefield. As she passed the bodies of the Elumerians, she reached down and wrenched off the manacle-shaped device that had projected the energy shield. "I've got a theory."

"We've got to get after Page," Burton said sharply.

"Agreed. Lieutenant, we can't stay here to assist you. We have orders—"

"Go on," she said. "I can jam this ship's signal for now. From the air, it'll look like we took each other out. I just need a little time to try something out."

Blackwelder felt a tug in his gut at the thought of leaving her behind, but he knew Burton was right; all of Fort Felix was at risk if they didn't stop Page. And if DeFrank were up to what he thought she might be up to, then her work would be equally important. He saluted her and gave the order for Brant Squad to march on.

Chapter Thirteen: Children of the Trident

"ADMIRAL VAUGHN," ABERNATHY said, "I have a secure channel open with Lieutenant DeFrank from the Narendra. I think she might have it, sir. She's testing it now."

"Best news I've heard all day, Captain. Tell her to keep at it and move quickly."

"Yes, sir."

"General Kilmer, Area Commander Zeng reports that E-Dome remains secure. They've taken heavy fire...three casualties...but the enemy has not been able to advance beyond the E-Dome corridor," Juan Miguel said.

"HQ, this is Lieutenant Colonel Lee. I've dispatched Bossa, Decker, Wilder, and Fen Squads to shut down the corridor access leading off to the M- and J-Domes. M-Dome corridor is reported secure. Awaiting confirmation on J-Dome."

Juan Miguel typed a command into the nearest monitor, and the view of the corridor leading from B-Dome to J-Dome appeared on screen. Bodies piled up at either end as the two advancing forces smashed into each other in the center of the long hallway. At the eye of the storm, several figures fought each other in melee combat; Greene, along with a few of his teammates from Wilder and Fen Squads, had abandoned their weapons and were taking on the Elumerians hand-to-hand. The aliens were taller and had a significant wingspan advantage, but Greene fought as if he were a much larger man. He tackled one of the Elumerians to the ground and smashed his helmet into the floor, shattering the creature's protective barrier and leaving it unable to breathe the air. The Elumerian spasmed violently for a moment and then ceased all movement. Greene got back to his feet, grabbed the nearest weapon, and surged forward, a push that seemed to inspire the others and opened a rift in the Elumerian front.

"I think...I think Greene just secured the J-Dome corridor," Juan Miguel said.

"Good. Our birds in the air are keeping their reinforcements off the ground. Tell them to keep holding the line at B-Dome," Kilmer said.

"Now let's hope your Brant Squad can handle Page, or else we all might as well be carving our own headstones," Vaughn said.

BLACKWELDER AND HIS team removed their helmets and space suits. They'd breached K-Dome's exterior door and had safely reestablished air and pressure. This of course meant that the Retribution were fully aware of their position, as a stealth entrance had been completely impossible.

Blackwelder turned to Petrey. "Are we good to go?"

"Yes, sir. I've reset all our coms to an alternating frequency. Their jammers shouldn't have any effect now."

"Good. Bailey, how's it look on your end?"

"They've overridden the lock sequence and fused the controls, sir." He'd opened the hatch near the wall and attached several wires connecting the panel to his own com device.

"How long 'til you get it open?"

Bailey considered for a moment, his eyes darting back and forth. "Four minutes, sir? Two minutes-thirty, if I'm very clever."

Blackwelder couldn't help but smile. "You've got two and half minutes, then."

He stared through a small window in the interior airlock door; Blackwelder could see Retribution agents moving quickly to set up a defensive perimeter. With no other way into the chamber, Brant Squad was going to have to walk directly into the line of fire.

"The one good thing about having to walk here was being able to load up the suits," Blackwelder said, pointing to the packs on the back of the space suits they'd all just discarded. To Burton, he said, "We're going to need a holo-cage defensive grid. Maximum coverage. They'll be shooting at us from all sides."

She nodded. "De Silva, Bonner, Petrey, cage stakes there, there, and there. Charge 'em up!"

Everyone moved quickly between the suit packs and the indicated locations to begin setting up the cage.

Blackwelder turned to Chiu. "And you?"

"I came prepared this time, sir." He pulled three grenades from his pack.

"Good man." He took notice of his crew as they set about carrying out his instructions. They'd been different since the brig, since war had unmistakably found each of them where they lived. They moved quickly but cautiously, and continuously looked to the other squad members; no one wanted to be the first to give in to the fear, which kept their spirits in line. He wanted to tell them not to worry, that their best would certainly be enough, but he couldn't tell that lie. Against heavily trained soldiers, united under zealous purpose? It would take everything they had and then some.

"Brant Squad," he called out. "Not that I need to remind you, but our mission is clear: we stop Arthur Page, whatever it takes. We're a team, and we'll do everything in our power to make sure everyone makes it out of here, but our priority, above all else, is Page. It's him or all of Fort Felix."

"The door's ready, sir," Bailey said.

"One last thing; I am incredibly proud to be serving with each and every one of you. I wouldn't want to be here with anyone else. Now let's go in there and get it done."

"Yes, sir!" they all chanted in unison. They took their positions behind the active holo-cages that were bunched together to create a solid barrier between Brant Squad and the interior door. They knelt down behind it, allowing the top portion of the screen to extend three quarters of the way above their heads, providing some essential cover.

Blackwelder gave the signal to Bailey. One swipe on his touch-com, and the heavy interior airlock doors ground open.

They were under attack immediately. Red laser blasts cascaded against the yellow-tinged walls of the holo-cage, sending orange sparks in all directions. Though the onslaught felt as if it were coming from everywhere at once, Blackwelder calmed himself and really took in the scene.

There were six men firing on them. Two shot from straight-on. They took cover behind the massive tech towers, heavily protected pillars that protruded from the ground like antennae. They were packed tight with cords and circuitry, and carried power and data to the far corners of Fort Felix. Slow-pulsing neon lights indicated that the tower was functioning properly. Two towers were set on either side of each of the ground-level workstations. There were ten of them, and at each one, a body lay lifeless on the ground.

Like the points of a star, the towers also radiated in straight lines away from the primary and secondary consoles, which is where their next two enemies were located. The platform for the secondary console rose about eight feet off the ground. A ramp wound around one side of the circular platform, while stairs spiraled tightly on the other. Pipes ran from its base along the same lines as the tech towers. On the platform, two Retribution agents had taken up positions, protected by the solid railing and some additional equipment they'd moved into place. Their elevation gave them a more accurate view of Blackwelder and his crew, but it put them farther away, making their shots more difficult.

The last two attackers had taken positions in the shadows of the equipment huts. There were four shedlike compartments in the dome that housed all manner of tools, two on either side of the room, and the Retribution traitors were firing from the two closest, which flanked Brant Squad. From the left, the right, straight-on, and from above, the Retribution fired on them.

After the couple heartbeats it took Blackwelder to observe them, he finally turned his attention to the primary console. It was shaped very similarly to the secondary console, but rose fifteen feet off the ground. At the top, Page typed furiously at a workstation, while the last two agents stood guard close by. Page seemed to somehow sense Blackwelder's attention on him.

Page raised his hand, and the Retribution's attack ceased.

"You and your misfit crew arrived a bit sooner than I expected, but as you can see, it's of no consequence," Page said, not looking up from his work. "It seems they knew I was coming and left me a randomizing tertiary encryption to distract me. Thanks to technology devised by some of the most brilliant hackers on Allied Earth, I will have it cracked in a matter of minutes."

"Was our system too advanced for your alien overlords? Or were you stuck with domestic because even they're confused by your inexplicable lust for the destruction of your own people?" Blackwelder said.

Page paused. He looked down to where Blackwelder huddled behind the decreasing safety of the holo-cage. "I have underestimated you, Blackwelder. I will concede that. But as I said before, you will not learn the secrets of the Retribution from me this day. And I wouldn't hold out hope for any other day either, given the state of your defenses."

Page waved his hand, and the attack began again in earnest. Under the constant barrage, the holo-cage was becoming overwhelmed, and the energy fields between the stakes rippled more intensely with each hit. Soon the stakes would be blasted apart and Brant Squad left defenseless.

"I think we need an exit strategy, sir," De Silva said, ducking.

Blackwelder quickly glanced down at his touch-com. "No. We need a distraction. Blackwelder to HQ! Come in HQ!"

"This is General Kilmer, son. Go ahead."

"General, we're pinned down and taking heavy fire in K-Dome. Page is using black market tech to crack the encryption on the defense controls. We need backup! Send anyone you can spare!"

Blackwelder, keeping his head low, turned back to his squad.

"Now, Chiu, I need you to hack the holo-cage and cross the refractory matrix with the energy synthesizer. Do you know what that will do?"

"Yes, sir, but—"

"Good. Wait for my signal. Bailey, can you jam Page's touch-com from here?" Blackwelder's fingers flew across the screen of his own device.

"Yes, sir. I can use the same frequency I used to get the doors open. It won't take him offline for long, though, especially if he's plugged into the console."

"I only need him down...three seconds. Can you give me that?"

"Yes, sir!" And minute later, Bailey was ready. Blackwelder nodded, and Bailey activated the com-hack. Immediately after him, Blackwelder clicked Send.

"I always keep a computer virus queued in my outbox. A trick a good friend taught me. She said one should never underestimate the usefulness of mail."

"What will it do?" Burton asked.

"If it works? Buy us time."

As if on cue, Page banged his fist into the desk. "No! What's happening?" He glanced over at Blackwelder.

"Hold your fire!" Page demanded. The Retribution ceased their assault on the holo-cage. "What have you done?"

Blackwelder smiled.

JUAN MIGUEL STARED at General Kilmer. "Every available soldier is currently flying around the base or keeping the Elumerians boxed in at B-Dome," Juan Miguel said. "They need help now."

"What do you propose?" Kilmer asked.

Juan Miguel locked gazes with Vaughn, Tsui, and Abernathy in turn. Then he jumped down from the central platform and ran over to the nearest analyst.

"I need your sidearm, please," Juan Miguel said to the man.

Senator Arías, who had been, for the most part, silently observing the battle, finally spoke up. "What do you think you're doing?"

"What needs to be done," Juan Miguel said.

As the soldier handed over his weapon, Abernathy jumped down and said, "I'm coming too."

"Dammit," Colonel Tsui said. "Gautier, Taal, you two go with them!"

As Juan Miguel and Abernathy sped up the stairs that would lead them out of the HQ, the two soldiers standing guard at the door turned and exited alongside them.

"What the hell was that, Kilmer," the senator spat.

"Fort Felix is the ambassador's home, the same any of the rest of us. And he has just as much right to fight for that home. Or are we so deep in our bounty that we can afford to deny able-bodied men who wish to serve?"

PAGE LEANED OVER the railing of the primary console. "For the second time, what have you done? If I am forced to ask again, then I will make sure your squad dies in agony."

"It's a computer virus," Blackwelder said after taking an unusually long breath. "I assume you know what those do?"

"You try my patience!" Page shouted.

"You linked your touch-com into the console to run your decryption program. I emailed you a virus that shuts down your com's functions. No more com, no more decryption program," Blackwelder said.

"Fix it. Now," Page demanded.

"You're the clever hacker. I'm sure you can sort it out." He'd angled himself so that he could face Page on his left, but his shoulders were still mostly perpendicular and facing forward. Blackwelder covertly slipped up one finger behind his back; Chiu blinked.

Page stared at him for a cold moment. "Rupture the ethylbenzene tanks and burn them alive," he said calmly.

"But, sir, if we do that, we will be trapped as well," said one of Page's guards.

"So be it. The mission is more important than any one of us."

"He's insane," De Silva said.

"Sir, wait," Page's other guard said. "The decryption algorithm is overwriting the virus and reasserting itself."

"It seems we all live to fight another day," Page said. "Well, most of us."

"Security Protocol FX-K6599 override accepted," said a monotone female voice from the console. "Base security grid restored to manual control."

"Page! Page, don't do this!" Blackwelder said.

An alarm blared to life as a red light flashed at the door that connected K-Dome to the A-Dome corridor.

"Shoot dead anything that comes through that door." Page hurried back to the console. "Deactivate all security fields," he yelled at the screen.

His Retribution traitors tried to reconfigure themselves to keep Brant Squad pinned down while also targeting the door at their backs, but before they could settle on secure offensive footing, the door was blasted from the wall in a shower of sparks. Juan Miguel strode into K-Dome, his borrowed sidearm poised and ready.

"Page!" he said, before opening fire. His shots were immediately doubled, tripled, and quadrupled by Abernathy and the HQ guards.

Blackwelder couldn't have planned it better; it was exactly the distraction he'd been waiting for.

"Now!" Blackwelder said.

Chiu crossed a pair of wires he'd pulled loose from one of the holo-cage stakes. The effect was immediate: the energy field, which locked the stakes together and provided Brant Squad with its lifesaving cover, spiked, sending golden arcs of electricity surging outward in four directions. Two of the blasts crashed against a tech tower, sparing the Retribution fighters hiding behind it. One of them cracked and sizzled the ground at the feet of the traitor crouching in the shadow of an equipment shed. But the fourth found a target, lifting the enemy soldier on their right a foot off the ground before slamming him mercilessly into the wall behind him.

With the holo-cage rendered completely useless, Brant Squad scattered to the left and right to avoid the head-on attack that was resuming. The Retribution fighters stationed on the secondary console opened fire; though he'd taken cover, Bailey was still partially exposed. He caught a laser blast in his right shoulder, which spun him around and left him out in the open. Defenseless, Bailey was hit with several more laser blasts before falling to the ground, dead.

"Bailey!" Petrey yelled, but Chiu prevented him from dashing into the crossfire to retrieve his friend.

Blackwelder lobbed one of Chiu's grenades into the traitors' nest. The resultant explosion ripped them from their perch and flung their bodies across the dome.

Focused in his anger, Blackwelder fired quickly now, taking out the guard still lurking to their left and training his weapon instead on Page, whose personal backup turned their weapons on Blackwelder. He fired up and landed several good shots, but the primary console was simply providing too effective a cover. Behind him, Blackwelder could hear Juan Miguel and his crew exchanging fire with those last two Retribution traitors on the ground level. There was an agonized groaning as Gautier, one of the HQ guards, crumpled to the ground.

"You have entered a Level 10 command request. Please enter Level 10 access code," the console said.

Ducking Blackwelder's attempts to take him out at a distance, Page typed furiously into his touch-com.

"Cover me," Blackwelder said to Burton and De Silva, who had slid into the shadow of the tool compartment at his side. They stood and immediately unleashed a stream of laser blasts that gave Blackwelder a slim window in the Retribution's defensive attack.

He ran full tilt toward a tech tower, hooking his arm around one side and slinging his body toward the ramp that wrapped around the side of the primary console. He ran up, almost tripping forward on the incline. He sped around the loop, which took him away from the action for a brief moment—a fraction of time that was eerily silent—before emerging on the same level as Page and his men. Not even pausing to breathe, Blackwelder shot one of Page's guards directly in the chest, sending him toppling over the railing. The other man countered, though, forcing Blackwelder to take cover behind a door that led to a maintenance hatch in the console.

"Level 10 access code accepted. Deactivating security fields in ten, nine, eight…" The console counted down to their destruction with an automated nonchalance.

Frustrated, Blackwelder yelled, "Think about what you're doing, Page!"

"Trust me, I've given this a great deal of thought," Page said. Staying just out of Burton and De Silva's line of fire, Page nodded his guard in Blackwelder's direction.

"—two, one—command halted. Senatorial override accepted," the console said.

"What? Senatorial—" Page began. They all looked across the way to see Juan Miguel standing at one of the remote workstations, surrounded by Abernathy and Bonner, as Taal and Petrey closed ranks on the two Retribution fighters on the ground level.

"It's over, Page," Blackwelder said.

Page whipped around to see his last guard, hands above his head. Chiu, with considerable stealth, had come up the staircase and disarmed him. Blackwelder fired a laser blast into the console, the explosion forcing Page to take several steps back.

"In case you got any ideas," Blackwelder said. And then, as if remembering, he said, "Bonner, check on Bailey!"

Page's face, first boiling with rage, seemed to calm quickly. Blackwelder could see the shift in his body, his shoulders flexing as he raised his right arm. It was as if he was back in the main hangar, watching Page zero in on the admiral again. He followed Page's gaze, only this time it wasn't Admiral Vaughn in his crosshairs.

Juan Miguel. Even the instant it took Blackwelder to think his name was an instant too long. The shot was already leaving Page's weapon. Juan Miguel was struck in the chest, and intense pain and very real surprise splashed across his face.

Blackwelder's eyes darted back to Page. The same surprise streaked Blackwelder's face when he saw Page standing still, lifeless; a blackened laser burn was positioned just above his eyebrow line. Blackwelder couldn't understand; he hadn't heard a second shot. Page's body leaned slowly forward, teetered for a minute, then tipped over the side of the railing and broke against the cold hard floor of K-Dome. With Page down, Blackwelder could see what he hadn't heard earlier: Burton stood over Page's body, her sidearm still smoking from the blast.

Juan Miguel had fallen to the ground by the time Blackwelder rushed to his side. His eyes were closed and his breathing was quick and shallow. Blood crept eerily across his white dress shirt.

"Come on, baby, wake up. Wake up! Bonner!"

She was already going to work. Bonner pulled the second of her two syringes from her pack. She plunged the needle into Juan Miguel's arm, then activated her touch-com to run a medical scan.

"He's losing a lot of blood. De Silva, check the emergency locker in the equipment shed and bring me the med-kit." She spoke and moved with a precision Blackwelder couldn't fully remember seeing from her before. It was a level of skill hinted at but never quite fully displayed.

De Silva returned with the kit. Bonner pointed to a spot at Juan Miguel's side directly across from her and in front of where Blackwelder sat, clutching Juan Miguel's hand. With an apologetic wince, De Silva boxed Blackwelder out, forcing him to let go of Juan Miguel's hand.

Bonner moved swiftly between Juan Miguel and the kit. She gave orders that De Silva seemed to be following, but Blackwelder wasn't quite sure; their voices were drowned out by a singular ringing tone. It pierced straight through Blackwelder's thoughts. He tried to watch them work, but his gaze slipped down to Juan Miguel's face. Juan Miguel's eyes were closed, and for the briefest of moments, he imagined that they were just in bed. That he had just woken up before Juan Miguel again and decided to watch him sleep. At any moment, those amber eyes would drift open and peer straight through him. But the ringing in his head, like an alarm, wouldn't allow the fantasy to continue.

Blackwelder had hesitated. The thought of Juan Miguel in mortal danger had paralyzed him, rather than spurred him to instantaneous action. He'd been extraordinarily fast in defending Vaughn, a man who'd shown him some measure of professional respect, especially considering his promotion, but who had also insinuated his disapproval of Blackwelder's personal expression. But when it had come to Juan Miguel, a man he was very much in love with, it was as if he'd forgotten all his skill, all his training, even if just for a fraction of a second.

A loud beeping sound ripped Blackwelder from his dark introspection.

"We're losing him! Attach the Fibs and stand back," Bonner said.

De Silva placed two flat black discs over Juan Miguel's heart and pushed back, creating a circle of space around him.

"Clear!" she said, tapping her touch-com. With a zapping sound, the black discs emitted a quick flash of blue electricity. Juan Miguel's body gave a small bounce, but otherwise nothing happened.

"Again, clear!" She tapped the screen again, and Juan Miguel's body jerked absently. But he did not open his eyes. Bonner pressed it once more, and the black discs zapped him a third time.

"Please, please." Blackwelder pushed past De Silva and grabbed Juan Miguel's hand again. "Stay with me," he whispered. "I'm so sorry."

De Silva was about to stop Blackwelder, but Burton waved him off. She gave a solemn nod to Bonner, who tapped her touch-com one last time, fully deactivating the discs and the flat-lined heart monitor that had been screaming out. A painful silence engulfed the room.

Still gripping Juan Miguel's hand, Blackwelder leaned in close so his lips were next to Juan Miguel's ear.

"I love you, Juan Miguel. I love you in more ways than there are stars in this universe, and if you come back to me, I swear I will name each and every one of them. Please," he whispered, "don't leave me."

Blackwelder rocked back and forth on his knees as he pressed his lover's hand to his chest. He could feel all of their eyes staring at him, every person in the room wondering what Blackwelder was about to do, now that his boyfriend was dead.

And then, in his hand, Blackwelder felt Juan Miguel's finger twitch. His hand lightly spasmed twice more, before finally returning Blackwelder's grip with force.

"I will hold you to that," Juan Miguel said weakly.

"I meant every word," Blackwelder said. He kissed Juan Miguel— gently, intently. A fraction of an instant later, though, the smile faded completely.

"Bailey," Blackwelder said, remembering.

"He's gone, sir," De Silva said. Behind them, Chiu and Petrey were attending to their fallen teammate's body.

"Dammit." Blackwelder felt the small bit of joy he'd managed at Juan Miguel's survival quickly slip away.

"I have news," Abernathy said. She was holding one finger to her ear while she watched her view screen. Once she had everyone's attention, she slid her fingers along the touch-com, and the volume projected so all of them could hear. The monitor at the closest workstation sprang to life, projecting an image of the six combatant warships still in their deadly face-off.

"That's confirmed, Captain Macke," Vaughn's voice said through the com. "Lieutenant DeFrank was able to use a functioning manta ship to access their shield codes, and found a way to deactivate them. She tested it on one of their personal shield devices. We have the interrupt sequence queued and ready to launch."

"They will scramble the code and get their shields back up. They will only be down a matter of seconds," Macke said.

Blackwelder shook his head. It seemed as if a lifetime had passed since he last heard that voice.

"Then you will have a matter of seconds, Captain. Make them count."

On screen, wave after wave of the fighters began to break off from their individual skirmishes and reform around the three Allied Earth ships.

"This is General Kilmer. All Fort Felix Cam fighters, form up on Captain Macke. Target all surface weapons on their starships."

"Malia, Narendra, Keqiang, fire everything you've got when we give the signal," Vaughn said.

"Launch the interrupt sequence, Colonel Tsui," Kilmer said.

"Interrupt sequence launched, sir. Shield deactivation in five, four, three, two, one..."

Just as it had when the Barack crashed into it headlong, the invisible fields surrounding the Elumerian starships began to visibly waver and disintegrate. In that instant, they were utterly defenseless.

"Fire," General Kilmer said.

Macke's Theta Squadron—or rather, what was left of it at that point—led the charge alongside a dozen other equally battered squadrons as they pushed their way through the throngs of manta ships. Macke pitched and rolled hard to the right, avoiding a wave of mantas and directed all his firepower toward the larger Elumerian starship closest to him.

"Keep attacking the starships!" Macke yelled, as Cam after Cam fell to well-placed manta blasts.

Thick bursts ripped from the cannons on Triton's surface and sailed unimpeded through the lack of atmosphere to find their prey. Without their shields to protect them, though, each and every blast found its target. Explosions rocked the surface of the Elumerian ships.

The Narendra launched a missile at one of the enemy starships. It was sleek and silver in its long casing, and even on screen, the missile glinted just so as it reflected light from the firefight mixed with a faint remnant from the sun. No commander in his right mind would have led the attack with one of those missiles. Not without knowing for sure the shield interruption had been successful. Even now, knowing the shields could come back online at any moment, it was a significant risk.

The nuclear missile floated across the screen, silently racing toward its target. With the shields still down, the missile made impact with the farthest Elumerian starship. In a blinding white light, the enemy vessel was ripped apart. A large chunk of the ship dislodged and flew into the next Elumerian ship, causing visible explosions there that left them apparently dead in the water.

"Their shields are back online, sir," Colonel Tsui said.

Their shields had reasserted themselves, but the coordinated attack had been a great success. With two ships completely destroyed and the third being abandoned, the last remaining ship, itself badly damaged, turned and pulled away from Triton/Neptune space. It generated a wave distortion, reopening the wormhole that had brought it, and returned to the depths of space.

"Attention Fort Felix: the Elumerian vessels have either retreated or been destroyed. The remaining Elumerians in this sector are now our prisoners. This battle is won!" General Kilmer said. Through the com, cheers of the men and women stationed in the HQ could be heard, cheers Blackwelder imagined were being echoed in every corner of the base. They were cheers he knew would sour as Fort Felix came to understand all that it had lost that day.

"SERGEANT MAJOR," BLACKWELDER said as Burton approached him. He was wearing his full dress-gray uniform, hat and all, and cut quite the handsome figure. More so, perhaps, because of the new insignia shining on his shoulder: a wide silver bar with two black stars. He stood in D-Dome, the main hangar bay, which still bore most of the scars of the recent battle, including scorch marks and blast residue, and repair scaffolding. A new shuttle had been sent to collect Admiral Vaughn, and what was left of his security detail was helping to prepare it for departure.

"You asked to see me, sir?"

"Yes. I wanted to say thank you for being a woman true to her word. Arthur Page never got to step foot off this base again." He extended his hand. "For Wyatt, and for Bailey."

She nodded but didn't say anything.

Blackwelder continued. "I regret to admit that I doubted whether or not you'd be able to stay on mission, or if you would go off desperate for revenge. You actually performed better than I did when it came down to it."

"We never know exactly how we'll react to seeing those we care about hurt. We think we do, but until we're in the moment, there's no way to be sure. We're all just doing the best we can, and there's no shame in that."

"Still, you avenged all three of them. I will always be grateful to you for that."

"How is he?"

"Our daring ambassador will pull through. He sustained a little damage to his left lung, but miraculously, the blast missed his spinal column by less than a millimeter. He's got some recovery time ahead of him, but he'll be just fine."

"That's good."

"And you? How are you?"

She stiffened a bit. "I will manage. We've all got a little recovery time ahead of us."

"That we do."

"I should get back to J-Dome. Was there anything else?"

"No. Thank you."

"Chief," Burton said, with a nod as she exited. She crossed paths with Abernathy, who was on her way to see Blackwelder as well.

"So, you're all set?" Blackwelder asked.

"We are. With the Barack gone, Admiral Vaughn has decided to move his command to the Keqiang. Since everything we had on the Barack was destroyed, General Kilmer is sending us off with a few extra provisions to help us get settled on the new ship."

"That's nice of him. He is certainly scuttling out of here quickly."

"Things are...prickly between the general and the admiral, which made the general's generosity uncomfortably awkward."

"What happened?"

"The admiral wanted to execute the captured Elumerians and the general insisted they be treated according to wartime conventions. I believe his exact words were 'If you don't like it, you can get the hell off my moon.'"

Blackwelder let out a small laugh. "Kilmer's a good man. And Fort Felix is a great place because of it."

"I agree. Especially for you, Chief Warrant Officer. I was thrilled to hear the general arranged a new warrant for you. You and your squad saved us all."

"Yes, well, how does that old saying go? No good deed goes unpunished."

"Truer words, old friend."

Unnoticed in his approach, Macke surprised Blackwelder. The tension spiked as they had not stood so close to one another in what seemed like a lifetime. Finally, Macke threw his arms around Blackwelder.

"It's good to see you, Spencer."

"Uh...yeah, you too, Robby. I really never thought—"

"Me neither," Macke said. "I understand you and Lyta have had a bit of a chat?"

"You could say that. I believe we've cleared the air. Right?"

"Yes," Abernathy said, taking Macke's hand. "We're sorry about Corporal Bailey. Everyone seemed to hold him in very high regard."

"We literally couldn't have done it without him. Likewise for your squadron, Mack. I understand you lost several brave pilots."

"Gone but never forgotten," Macke said.

Blackwelder looked around. The damage was severe, but there was something inspiring in the work of repair. "We actually won this today, despite the heavy losses. But they'll be back, and soon." He considered his next words carefully, lowering his voice. "And it won't be with four ships next time."

"No, it won't. But we'll be ready for them. Because we'll have to be. It looks like we're ready to go," Abernathy said, as one of Vaughn's men waved them over.

"I'm glad you came here. It's was good to see you both."

"Me too, Spencer. And tell Juan Miguel he should maybe be a little less heroic next time," Abernathy said.

"I'll tell him, but I doubt he'll listen."

Abernathy and Macke headed off to the waiting shuttlecraft. They stepped in line just behind Admiral Vaughn. Vaughn, catching sight of Blackwelder, nodded briefly. For his part, Blackwelder saluted the admiral as they all boarded their ship. As he brought his hand down, Blackwelder noticed the Fort Felix emblem on the floor. The base had endured much, but the golden trident and white stars still shone brightly, a promise to those who would rally behind it. A promise that, despite the failings of men, or whatever monsters might emerge from the deep, they would always endure.

About the Author

Christopher D. J. was born and raised in the South, calling multiple cities home between North Carolina, South Carolina, and Florida, but none more so than Daytona Beach, where he graduated from Mainland High School. Christopher went on to complete his BA at Duke University and his MPW at the University of Southern California. Christopher is the author of Blackwelder: 2164 and Between Two Brothers. He briefly worked in the entertainment industry before turning his attention full-time to higher education; he currently has the pleasure of serving first-year students and families at California State University, Los Angeles as the Assistant Director for New Student and Parent Programs.

Christopher lives in Los Angeles, CA, where he enjoys comic books, movies, cheeseburgers, French fries, and not having to worry about mosquitoes.

Facebook: www.facebook.com/ChristopherDJFiction/

Twitter: @StopherJo

Instagram: www.instagram.com/StopherJo

Pinterest: www.pinterest.com/christopherdj

Also Available from NineStar Press

Connect with NineStar Press

www.ninestarpress.com

www.facebook.com/ninestarpress

www.facebook.com/groups/NineStarNiche

www.twitter.com/ninestarpress

www.tumblr.com/blog/ninestarpress

www.ingramcontent.com/pod-product-compliance
Lightning Source LLC
Chambersburg PA
CBHW051705180726
48283CB00004B/1216